Suddenly Mandy began to feel uncomfortable. It was as if someone was watching her. Glancing around the room, her gaze was drawn to the window. Mandy felt her body go rigid and held her breath. It was there! The wolf was there! It was staring right at her . . .

This time, it couldn't possibly be her imagination. The wolf was enormous – Mandy could see its great mane of white fur shining in the moonlight. And its gaze was so intense that it seemed to bore right into her . . . She stared back at the wolf, not daring to look away for an instant, in case it disappeared.

'Mandy!' She could hear her mother calling to her. Mandy didn't want to move, even to nod her head.

'Dad's suggesting we go to the wildlife park tomorrow,' Mrs Hope said and laughed. 'Would you like to go, or is that a silly question?'

Mandy knew she had to respond. For a brief second she dragged her gaze away from the sad, yellow eyes of the great wolf to nod agreement to her mum.

But when she looked back, the wolf was gone.

LUCY DANIELS

Wolf
— *at the* —
Window

Illustrations by Ann Baum

*Hodder
Children's
Books*

a division of Hodder Headline

Special thanks to Tanis Jordan
Thanks also to C. J. Hall, B.Vet.Med., M.R.C.V.S., for reviewing
the veterinary information contained in this book.

Animal Ark is a trademark of Working Partners Ltd
Text copyright © 2000 Working Partners Ltd
Created by Working Partners Ltd, London W6 0QT
Illustrations copyright © 2000 Ann Baum
Original series created by Ben M. Baglio

First published in 2000
by Hodder Children's Books

A Catalogue record for this book is available from the British Library

ISBN 0 340 78809 7

Typeset by Avon Dataset Ltd, Bidford-on-Avon, Warks

Printed and bound in Great Britain by
Clays Ltd, St Ives plc

Hodder Children's Books
A Division of Hodder Headline Limited
338 Euston Road
London NW1 3BH

One

'Hurry up and close the door,' Adam Hope joked as Mandy Hope and her friend James Hunter struggled in, carrying between them a big basket of logs and putting it by the fireplace. 'You're letting all the cold in.'

'And all the heat out,' Emily Hope added, looking up from her book and winking at her husband.

'Is *that* all the thanks we get?' Mandy asked, sitting down and pulling off her wellingtons. She pretended to sound indignant. 'It's freezing out there *and* it's starting to snow.'

'It's coming down in really big flakes,' James

said, 'and they're beginning to settle.'

'All the more reason to fetch the logs, then,' said Mandy's dad. 'Anyway, you two are young and energetic. Mum and I are old and tired.'

'Not so much of the "old" if you don't mind, Adam,' Mandy's mum said haughtily, raising her eyebrows and looking sideways at her husband. 'I'll certainly agree with the "tired" though. I don't think we've ever been quite so busy as in the last few weeks. It seems like we've treated nearly every animal in Yorkshire!'

'That's because you're the best vets around,' Mandy told them with a grin. 'Everyone wants to come to Animal Ark.' Animal Ark was the Hopes' thriving veterinary practice in the Yorkshire village of Welford.

'Not this weekend, I hope,' Emily Hope said, raising her eyebrows. 'We don't want Simon and Alistair snowed under with work.' Simon was the practice nurse at the surgery. He and Alistair King, the locum vet, were holding the fort while the Hopes were away in Scotland.

'I think we might be snowed under instead,' Adam Hope observed, looking out of the window.

The birthday invitation from Adam Hope's

old college friend had arrived last month. Angus Mudie was celebrating his fortieth birthday with a huge party. Mandy had been really excited, as the invitation included her and a friend.

'Turn it over and read the back,' Adam Hope had suggested.

' "Why not come up to the majestic Scottish Highlands and stay a few days to unwind?" ' Mandy had read aloud. ' "You can see the wildlife park that I helped set up." ' She looked at her dad, eyes shining with anticipation. 'Dad, can we go? Can I take James?'

'I don't see why not,' Mr Hope had responded. 'Mum and I could use a break.'

Of course, Blackie, James's Labrador, had come too. While most of the other party guests would stay in the main house, which was split into modern self-catering apartments, the Hopes had taken advantage of the peace and quiet of the old gamekeeper's lodge.

Now, after a long drive, they were relaxing beside a roaring log fire in the cosy living-room. The lodge was a solid building, made from thick blocks of stone and with a big oak door. Though it had been modernised, it still had the original furniture, with paintings dotted around the rooms. The front door opened into the hall and the back door straight into the kitchen in which there was a wood-burning range that heated the house. Someone from the main house had come in and lit the fire and put fresh sheets on the beds before they'd arrived. Angus had even left a welcome hamper for them in the kitchen. Mandy's parents' bedroom was full of pictures of birds. Two tiny bedrooms had been built in what had once been a loft.

'Where can Blackie sleep?' James asked in a worried voice when they carried their bags up and Mandy pushed open the doors.

'Hmm,' Mandy said, as she studied the tiny rooms. 'If we move your bedside table and push the bed against the wall he could just squeeze in.' Together they heaved the bed against the wall and made a space for Blackie.

Mandy and James's bedrooms were reached by a steep, winding staircase in the middle of the house. These rooms had small square windows that creaked open sideways, but the downstairs windows were larger and made of several panes of glass. They were set in the stone and weren't made to be opened at all.

Mr Hope settled back comfortably in his chair. 'This is the life,' he sighed. 'Now, if *someone* would make us a nice cup of tea, everything would be just fine,' he said, looking pointedly at Mandy.

'OK,' Mandy said. 'I can take a hint, Dad.'

'Your dad says that he's feeling a bit peckish too,' James told Mandy as he joined her in the kitchen. 'So am I, actually.'

'When *aren't* you hungry, James?' Mandy teased, laughing as James turned pink.

'When I'm asleep?' wondered James.

'Right,' Mandy said purposefully. 'Let's see what we can find.' She opened the wicker hamper Angus had left.

'Wow!' said James, his eyes lighting up.

There was a loaf of crusty bread, a huge slab of butter, half a dozen little jars of assorted jams and marmalades, a box of shortbread and a packet that said 'Genuine Scottish Oatcakes'.

Mandy made a pot of tea, poured some milk into a jug and set them both on a tray with four mugs.

'Will you take the tray through, please, James?' she asked. 'I'll just look for some plates.'

'OK,' said James, picking up the tray.

Mandy held the door open for him and James crossed the hall, heading for the living-room. She had just turned back into the kitchen when the light started to flicker and then went out completely, plunging the kitchen into darkness. Almost immediately Mandy heard the crash of crockery breaking. James must have dropped the tray.

Mandy stood still and tried to get her bearings in the dark. It was pitch black; too dark to see her hand in front of her face. It was probably just a power cut, she thought. Perhaps they happened quite often here. She remembered that there were candles in most of the rooms.

Mandy stood very still and gradually became aware of a noise. She held her breath. In the dead silence, she could hear a faint gulping sound that seemed to be coming towards her. She wasn't alone. There was someone or *something* in the room with her.

She gripped the table hard and tried to stop the shivers that were running up and down her spine. She could feel her heart pounding – it felt like it was in her throat. She tried to convince herself that old houses made strange noises. Something touched her foot. Slowly and carefully she bent down to feel what it was. Her hand came in contact with cold, clammy skin.

'Aaaagh!' Mandy yelled loudly. She almost fell over backwards as the creature leaped away. At that moment the lights came back on and Emily Hope charged into the room, followed by James.

'What happened, Mandy?' she asked in a worried voice. 'We heard you shout.'

'I don't know,' Mandy said, pulling a face. 'Something was on my foot and when I touched it, it jumped up. Its skin was all rough and sort of warty.'

Adam Hope was standing in the doorway holding the tray of crockery and trying to look innocent. 'I think you've just met Mr Buffo,' he told Mandy. 'He's a rather large toad who lives under the sink. He's been there some years. Angus mentioned him when I phoned to accept the invitation. I forgot to tell you.'

'I bet you did, Dad!' Mandy said.

James went over to the sink and moved the checked curtain that hung round its base. Sitting contentedly on the bottom shelf next to a bottle of floor cleaner was a very big toad. It blinked at them reproachfully.

'He's really pretty!' said Mandy. 'Look at his amber eyes.'

'I don't think you describe a toad as pretty,' James pointed out.

'Handsome, more likely,' Adam Hope said, as he put the tray of crockery on the table. 'Only one breakage, but we'll need some more tea, please. And look what I found by the fireplace!' He held up a fork with a great long handle. 'It's a toasting fork. Why don't I slice that loaf and we can toast it in front of the fire?'

Soon a delicious smell of toasting bread filled the air. They tried the oatcakes too, with butter and jam on them, and almost finished off the shortbread.

'If I can find some real oatmeal in that kitchen,' Adam Hope said, as Mandy took his empty plate away, 'I'll make us some proper Scottish porridge in the morning. If I remember rightly, you have to soak it overnight.'

'I noticed that Angus has left a pair of kippers in the fridge,' Mrs Hope told her husband. 'The label says that they were smoked on the Mudie Estate.'

'Would they have been caught in the lake?' James asked, giving an involuntary shiver. 'I bet it's deep.'

'Loch,' Adam Hope told him. 'Lakes are called lochs in Scotland and it certainly will be deep, and cold. Angus used to say that it was often too cold to swim in, even in summer. Welford seems positively warm by comparison to the Mudie Estate,' he added. 'Talking of which, would you put another log on the fire, please, James? And to answer your question about the fish, they could well have come out of the loch. It's a seawater loch, even though we're quite a way inland.'

James dropped a log on the fire, sending

sparks flashing up the chimney and into the hearth. Blackie, who had been curled up on the rug in front of the fire, leaped up excitedly, snapping at the fiery flying lights.

'Look out, Blackie!' Mandy called as she and James lunged to grab the dog. But they were too late. With a soft sizzle a spark landed directly on Blackie's wet black nose. He yelped in surprise and ran straight behind a sofa.

'Oh, Blackie, you poor thing,' Mandy said, as she and James got down on all fours to examine Blackie's nose.

'Let me have a look,' Mrs Hope said, quickly putting her book down and standing up. 'I hope the sparks didn't get in his eyes.'

'Come on, Blackie, out you come,' James said, pulling gently at the dog's collar.

Mandy tried to help, but Blackie resisted all their efforts to coax him from behind the sofa.

'It's no good, he won't budge,' James told Mrs Hope.

'Let me have a look at him,' Mrs Hope said, kneeling down in their place and peering behind the sofa. 'Hmm, that'll be fine in a couple of days. It probably stung at the time, which is why he yelped,' she told them. 'His eyes are OK – no problems there.' She ruffled the top of Blackie's head and he looked up at them all sheepishly. 'It's his pride that's hurt more than anything,' Emily Hope said with a smile. 'He's embarrassed! I bet we won't see Blackie curled up in front of the fire for at least half an hour.'

Mandy smiled to herself as she watched James kneel down and whisper something softly in Blackie's ear. As soon as they'd arrived earlier that afternoon, she and James had taken Blackie to explore the estate. The lodge was high on a sloping bank above the loch, surrounded by pine and oak forests. Hills covered with mauve heather stood in the distance. Mandy, James and Blackie had come home when the snow had started to fall.

Now, Mandy looked across to the window to see if it had stopped snowing, but all she could see was the reflection of her dad and his reading lamp. She moved closer and shielded her eyes with her hands to block out the light. In the moonlight Mandy could see that although it was no longer snowing, a light dusting of white flakes covered everything.

Suddenly, as she leaned closer, she spotted a

pattern etched in the glass. She moved nearer, noticing that the etching seemed to be of an animal.

As her eyes grew accustomed to the darkness outside the window she began to make out the shape of the etching. It was an old dog – it looked like a German shepherd. The Mudie family must really love animals to have a picture of a dog etched in the window. But as she watched, she became puzzled. The dog's eyes looked so real, and they even seemed to be yellow. How had they done that? Suddenly, the whole picture in the window seemed to slip into a different focus. Mandy took a sharp breath.

It's not a picture, Mandy thought with a jolt. It's a *real* dog! There's a dog outside the window – it's looking in . . .

Mandy's first urge was to run outside to bring the dog into the warm. But she couldn't move. The animal's eyes held her. They bored into hers – it was almost as if they were trying to tell her something.

For what seemed like ages Mandy stood mesmerised. Then questions slowly formed in her mind. All of her experience with dogs told her that they didn't *have* yellow eyes. But this one did. And its head was really big – this dog must be enormous!

The creature's neck was so big and its coat so dense that there were rolls of fur round its neck, which looked like ruffs. Its fur was white, flecked with grey, and there was a dark grey stripe like a T across its forehead and down its muzzle.

Mandy wanted to turn round to call the others to look, but she still felt rooted to the spot.

Suddenly the creature stood up. As soon as it was upright and Mandy saw its long legs, she knew. It was a wolf. She felt a shiver start at the nape of her neck and slide down her spine.

Two

'Mandy?' Adam Hope called urgently. 'What's wrong? You're as white as a sheet.'

Mandy beckoned him, but her dad was already out of his chair and coming across the room towards her. She put her finger to her lips and silently mouthed the word 'wolf'.

Emily Hope and James looked out of the window with worried faces. But when Mandy turned back to the snowy scene, the wolf was gone. She stepped forward and rubbed the pane of glass with her arm, peering out to see if she could spot the creature walking away.

'It *was* there, honestly,' she said, staring out

anxiously. 'It was a big grey and white wolf with yellow eyes. I was watching it for ages. At first I thought it was a dog, but when it stood up its legs were far too long. And it was *huge* – its head was at least this big.' Mandy held her hands apart to demonstrate the size.

Emily Hope put her hand on Mandy's forehead. 'You *are* very pale, Mandy,' she said. 'Do you feel all right?'

'Mum, I *did* see it,' Mandy said in an urgent voice. She pressed her face against the cold glass of the window but everything outside was still.

'Sometimes the imagination plays tricks on us, Mandy,' Adam Hope said gently. 'Especially when we're tired. It's been quite a long day.'

Mandy squared her shoulders and looked up at her dad. 'I didn't imagine it, Dad. I *know* I saw it.'

'There'll be tracks, won't there?' James asked eagerly. 'Surely it would have left tracks?'

Mandy shot him a grateful look. At least James seemed to believe her. She dashed to the door, undid the bolt and pulled it open. Blackie sprang up and bounded to the door, his blister forgotten.

'Whoa there, Blackie,' James said, grabbing

his collar. 'I think you should stay inside if there's a wolf about.'

Mandy saw her parents exchange glances. She looked at the ground beyond the doorstep. There *were* some tracks there. But as Mandy followed the tracks with her eyes, she realised that they led to the woodpile.

'They're the footprints we made earlier,' James said softly, coming to stand beside her.

Mandy made her way carefully to the outside of the window where she'd seen the wolf. There wasn't a single mark on the snow-covered ground. She couldn't believe it. She touched the window. It was dry. There was no mark where the wolf's breath would have clouded the cold glass. She looked at the patch of ground where the wolf had stood. It was covered by crisp new snow.

Mandy felt her dad's hands on her shoulders and looked up at him. 'Face it, love,' he said, giving her a lopsided grin. 'There haven't been any wolves in Scotland for hundreds of years. It must have been a trick of the light, maybe a reflection from the lamps or something. These things happen.'

'But Dad, that's what I saw first, the lamp's

reflection. That's why . . .' Mandy broke off. She looked from one to the other. She could see from their faces that they thought she'd imagined it, and she didn't know how to convince them. She took a deep breath and sighed. 'OK, maybe you're right,' she admitted grudgingly. But in her heart of hearts, Mandy *knew* that she'd just seen a wolf.

'Let Blackie out to have a little run now, and then I suggest an early night would do us all good,' Emily Hope said in a cheerful voice. 'I'm exhausted.' She stifled a yawn and pushed open the front door into their holiday home. Blackie was snuffling impatiently at the door and rushed out, almost knocking Mrs Hope over in the process.

'Sorry,' James apologised, and quickly threw a stick for Blackie. Mandy giggled as James's dog hurtled after the stick, leaping up in the air with excitement.

'You've got so much energy, Blackie,' laughed Mandy as the Labrador dropped the stick at James's feet.

As James threw the stick again, Mandy did the same with another from the woodpile. Confused, Blackie skidded to a halt, then dashed after Mandy's stick.

Mandy grinned and then quickly looked back at the window. There was absolutely nothing to be seen. If an animal had been there, she realised with a shudder, it had left no trace at all.

'I think that's tired him out,' James said, coming to stand beside Mandy. She heard Blackie panting as he ran up to them. But instead of bringing James the stick, the dog stopped and dropped it a short distance away from them, his tail firmly between his legs. No amount of coaxing from James could make him come any closer. 'He can be so stubborn,' James said, shaking his head. 'Let's go in – he'll soon follow us.'

Sure enough, as they reached the front door Blackie ran up to them wagging his tail.

'You silly dog,' James said fondly, rubbing Blackie's ears. 'When will you learn to behave properly?'

Maybe Blackie wasn't silly at all, Mandy thought later as she climbed the stairs to her bedroom. What if Blackie had sensed something outside? She knew that dogs' hearing was really sensitive. She yawned and climbed

into bed. Before she had had a chance to think about the wolf again she was sound asleep.

Next morning, Mandy woke up early to find that the snow had melted. A milky-white mist hung over the loch, lit by the first weak rays of the rising sun. It looked warmer than yesterday but, as Mandy flung open the window, she was met with a blast of cold air. As she hurried to close it again, there was a sudden movement among the trees on the other side of the loch.

Vivid memories of the wolf came flooding into Mandy's head and she froze as the mist swirled and cleared for a moment to reveal a figure in a blue tracksuit, bent over with his hands on his knees. Mandy grinned. Her dad was out jogging. She quickly pulled on some warm clothes and gently opened James's door.

James was asleep but Blackie opened one eye and looked at her.

'Come on, Blackie,' Mandy urged. 'Let's go and find Dad.' She ran downstairs, pulled on her wellingtons, grabbed her coat and dashed outside, with Blackie close at her heels. Sunlight was glinting on the loch as the mist shimmered away to nothing, and the cold, crisp air was full of birdsong.

Mandy glanced at the window where the wolf had been. Everything looked perfectly normal. *Could* she have imagined it? She had to admit that the wolf seemed unbelievable in the bright daylight. Mandy sighed to herself and ran around the loch towards her dad.

As Blackie went haring past, Adam Hope turned around and jogged backwards. 'Morning, love,' he greeted her, his breath puffing out like clouds of steam.

'Don't you think you might be overdoing it, Dad?' Mandy said, looking with concern at her dad's red face.

'I – *puff* – wanted – *puff* – to work up – *puff* – an appetite,' Mr Hope said as he slowed to a walk. 'Wait till you taste my real porridge!' He laid an arm across Mandy's shoulders and gave her a little hug. 'How do you feel this morning?'

'I'm fine, Dad.' Mandy smiled at him. 'Last night I was sure that I'd seen a wolf, but this morning, well . . .' She broke off and bit her lip. '*Something* was there, Dad, honestly.'

'Maybe there was, Mandy, maybe there was. After all we don't know the history of this place, do we?' Adam Hope said, looking at her thoughtfully as they reached the lodge and went inside. 'Anyway, let me loose in that kitchen. Breakfast will be ready as soon as I've jumped in the shower!'

When Mandy and James sat down at the table ten minutes later, it was set with three bowls. A large pot of porridge bubbled gently on the range.

Adam Hope placed a large, steaming bowl in front of Mandy. 'Sometimes, people dip the ladle in cream before serving,' he said filling a bowl for James, whose face lit up instantly.

'Mmmm,' murmured James.

'Sorry, we're out of cream. But we do have salt!' he laughed, passing Mandy the salt cellar. 'This makes it taste *really* nice.'

Mandy's mouth fell open. 'Ugh, that sounds horrible,' she said.

'James?' Mr Hope looked at James who had gone rather pink.

'Don't tease, Adam,' Emily Hope said from the doorway. She was smiling as she came into the room, her red hair still damp from the shower and curling in tendrils around her face.

She reached up into a cupboard and passed James a bowl of sugar.

'I think I'll stick with this for now,' James said, relief in his voice, as he tasted a spoonful of the porridge. 'This is delicious, Mr Hope.'

'Why, thank you, James,' Mr Hope said, putting a tea towel over his arm and giving a small bow. 'Compliments of the chef.'

'Speaking of food, would you mind going down to the shop for me?' Mrs Hope asked Mandy and James as she sat down. 'I brought some food with us, but we need fresh milk and fruit and you could maybe get some yoghurts.'

Mandy nodded. 'No problem,' she agreed cheerfully.

While Adam Hope ate his grilled kippers and Mandy and James washed up, Mrs Hope sat at the table writing a shopping list. 'You should be able to get everything at the mini-supermarket we passed yesterday,' she told them.

'I'll take Blackie,' James said to Mandy, 'but I'd better keep him on his lead if we're going by road.'

With James holding firmly on to Blackie's lead, they set off for the village. Before long the estate was behind them and a lonely road lay ahead.

The only vehicle to pass them on the way was a large green farm van with bales of hay sticking out through the back doors. When they arrived at the shop, it was parked outside.

Piled up near the entrance to the mini-supermarket were bags of coal and bundles of logs and kindling. Three Calor gas cylinders were roped together and tied to a metal ring attached to the wall. James tied Blackie's lead to the ring and told him to behave.

Inside the shop, Mandy took charge. 'If you get a basket, James, I'll find what we need,' she suggested. She'd found milk, cheese and locally made yoghurts and was just picking out some fruit when she heard raised voices.

'And I say it's all *wrong*!' a man's voice said loudly. 'They'll be nothing but trouble, you mark my words.'

Another man agreed. 'Aye, he's right. They don't belong here.'

'These foreigners and their stupid ideas . . . They should stop down south and mind their own business,' someone else added.

Mandy and James exchanged glances. 'Do you

think they're talking about us?' James whispered in alarm.

'Why should they?' Mandy said, her voice indignant. 'We haven't done anything wrong. Now what else is on the list? Right, where are the magazines?'

A huddle of people surrounded the magazine rack. A man wearing blue overalls and muddy boots was talking furiously and shaking his fist. His face was deep red with anger and the veins in his neck were pulsing. He banged his fist down on the counter, making Mandy and James jump and the till rattle.

'*I* won't put up with it,' he said, scowling. 'And nor will any farmer around here worth his salt, not when they read this.' He held a newspaper open to show the other customers the headline.

Mandy realised that he was standing right in front of the magazine she wanted and she stepped forward. 'Excuse me,' she said politely, trying to squeeze past him.

'It's a nonsense!' a tall man said. He was smartly dressed in a green waxed jacket and brown corduroy trousers. 'What about my deer? They'll be after them as soon as look at you. Not to mention the game birds.'

The man in the blue overalls whacked the newspaper, tearing the page. Mandy wondered what could have made him so cross. She looked at James who was choosing a computer magazine and trying to keep a low profile.

'Let me tell you one thing,' the man said in such a menacing voice that Mandy went cold. 'There'll not be wolves in Scotland while I live and breathe. Be sure of that, now.'

Wolves! Mandy could hardly believe her ears.

'Brett, don't you think you're taking it too much to heart?' said the shopkeeper as he weighed up some carrots. 'They're only young wolves and they'll be safe enough in the park. Angus and Duncan wouldn't do anything foolish.'

'Foolish!' Brett spat out the word, Mandy decided that his narrowed eyes looked really shifty. The man rolled the paper in his hand and held it like a truncheon in front of him. 'It was a dark day when they brought wolves back to these parts, I'm telling you. They may be young now, but they'll grow and what then? Eh? Those wolves will be trouble!' And with that he marched out of the shop and slammed the door.

'He's always been a hothead, has Brett

McCatter,' the shopkeeper said to the man in the corduroy trousers.

'He's a point there,' the man answered. 'It's a worry for any stockman in the area. Wolves are natural-born killers. I don't know what Mudie can be thinking about.'

'What about the bairns, I say?' a woman with a shawl over her coat said. 'It's said that in the old days, wolves would take a bairn if they could.'

Another woman nodded agreement. 'That's true.'

Gradually the people drifted away, muttering to each other as they left the shop, until only Mandy and James remained.

Mandy felt thoroughly confused. She couldn't work out what everyone was so worked up about, but it was definitely to do with wolves.

'Good morning! And what can I do for you?' the shopkeeper asked Mandy kindly. 'You're not from around these parts, are you?'

'We're from Yorkshire,' Mandy told him. 'We're staying in the gamekeeper's lodge on the Mudie Estate.'

'Then you'll be up for the ceilidh,' he said. 'It'll be a grand do.' He laughed at Mandy's frown. 'The birthday party, I mean. There'll be a lot of dancing going on!'

'Oh, yes,' Mandy agreed. 'But could you tell us what everyone was saying about wolves, please?'

'Don't worry your head about wolves,' said the shopkeeper, tutting. 'They're not going to be any bother at all.' He shook his head before continuing. 'Some people get themselves all worked up over nothing and they stir everyone else up while they're about it. Brett is always trying to cause trouble, one way or another . . .'

'But what's a *bairn*?' James asked. 'The lady said that a wolf took one.'

The shopkeeper laughed. 'A bairn is a child and some say that wolves would carry them away. But that's an old wives' tale. You don't want to listen to that nonsense. What's happened is that the wildlife park has just taken delivery of two young wolves.'

'Is that the wildlife park that Mr Mudie helped to set up? Mandy asked.

'The very same. And some of the local people are getting very worried about their livestock. *Not* that's there's any need to worry, in my opinion,' he said, taking the basket from James and beginning to add up the items. 'Duncan knows well enough how to keep his animals safely in their enclosures. They won't escape. All this talk of re-introducing the wolves into Scotland is jumping the gun. It's wrong of the newspapers to get everyone annoyed.'

He handed James the carrier bag. 'That's four pounds seventy. Thank you very much,' he said, taking the money Mandy offered. 'Why don't you go to the park and see the wolves? They're nice-looking creatures,' he added as they left the shop.

Mandy was thoughtful as they collected Blackie and walked down the road. Suddenly she stopped. 'Hang on, James,' she said. 'I won't be minute.' She turned and ran back to the shop, but it was empty. 'Excuse me,' she called urgently from the door.

'Have you forgotten something?' the shopkeeper asked, appearing from behind a beaded curtain that hung across a doorway.

'No, nothing,' said Mandy, her voice unsure. 'It's just that you did say *young* wolves, didn't you?'

'Aye, I did. They're not tiny cubs mind you – juveniles I think they call them,' he said.

'And there used to be wolves in Scotland?'

'Aye, there were,' the shopkeeper answered. 'More than enough. In the old days, the Highlands were rich in lots of wildlife that you don't see today.'

'Thank you,' Mandy said, as she closed the door. She couldn't help thinking of the huge grizzled old wolf at the window, staring at her with its amber eyes glowing.

Three

Mandy had been lost in thought since they'd left the shop.

'What's up?' James asked as they walked back along the road, with Blackie tugging at his lead.

'It's hard to explain,' Mandy began. 'It's just that, well, don't you think it's strange that I saw a wolf last night and today we find out that there actually *are* wolves near here.'

'Yes, but these are *real* ones,' said James, turning to look at Mandy.

Mandy stopped dead in her tracks and stared at James. 'You think I imagined it, too, don't you?' she said, her voice full of disappointment.

'No!' James said hesitantly, 'It just seems a bit weird, you know.' He shifted uncomfortably. 'No one else saw it – the wolf, I mean – and there weren't any tracks. There aren't any wolves around here anyway, except in the park – we'd have heard if they'd escaped.'

'OK,' Mandy said cautiously. 'Anyway, I suppose the wolf that I saw wasn't that young. It was huge and its eyes were old and sad.'

James opened his mouth to say something, then closed it again when Mandy gave him a look.

'And,' she carried on, 'who says that *all* the wolves in Scotland have disappeared? What if some survived and are living in the middle of the Highlands, where nobody knows about them?' Mandy was warming to her theory now. 'And what if one came to the window last night and I happened to see it!' she finished triumphantly, setting off again towards the lodge.

'It's possible, I suppose,' James said, looking doubtful. He knew better than to dismiss Mandy's idea out of hand. 'But why?' he asked carefully, almost jogging to keep up with her. 'I mean, why should it come and stare in the window?'

'Well, I don't know *why*,' Mandy argued. 'But it did! I *wish* I knew more about wolves.'

'That's easy,' James said, delighted to be on safer ground with Mandy. 'We can look it up! There must be a library somewhere around here . . .'

'Yep, there is,' Mandy replied, giving a firm nod. 'I'm sure I saw a sign in the village.'

'Then we can find out all we want to know about wolves there. Let's take the shopping back to the lodge and then go and investigate,' James suggested.

'Right,' Mandy agreed, feeling much happier. 'I'll race you up the drive.'

'That's not fair,' James grumbled good-naturedly. 'I'm carrying all the shopping. You've got Blackie and he loves to run!'

Mandy was out of breath when she reached the track that led from the main house to the lodge. She let Blackie off his lead and while he darted in and out among the trees, she sat on a log and waited for James.

'That wasn't fair,' James gasped, dropping down beside her on the log. He pointed to the shopping. 'Where's Bla—?'

Before James could finish his sentence, there was a huge commotion behind them. A rubber ball came bouncing down the path, closely followed by an excited Blackie. When he saw James, he didn't seem sure whether he should stop or carry on after the ball. James jumped up to grab him but Blackie was going too fast and they both ended up in a crumpled heap on the ground.

Mandy was still laughing when a boy who looked about twelve years old appeared round a bend in the track. Blackie ran to the boy and sat at his feet.

'He's a fine-looking dog,' the boy said politely. 'Is he yours?'

'No.' Mandy chuckled, pointing at James. '*That's* Blackie's owner!'

The boy looked quizzically at James, who was sitting, dishevelled, on the ground.

'He's mine,' James confirmed, pushing his glasses back on his nose. 'And he gets a bit . . .' He looked around for a word. 'Exuberant!' he exclaimed.

'Exactly!' Mandy agreed.

'My name is Cameron Mudie,' the boy said.

'And you two must be Mandy and James!'

'That's right,' Mandy responded. 'And this is Blackie.'

'We've met already in the woods,' Cameron said. 'I sent him chasing after the ball.'

'Have you got a dog too?' Mandy asked him.

'I have, and she loves chasing after that ball,' Cameron told them. 'She's quite old now and it's the only way I can make her take exercise.'

'She's not a big German shepherd, is she?' Mandy asked cautiously.

'Goodness, no,' Cameron said with a laugh. 'She's a little brown mongrel called Beattie. Why do you ask?'

'Mandy thought she saw one last night.' James offered a simple explanation.

Cameron bent down and stroked Blackie with a thoughtful look on his face. 'I can't think of anyone around here with a German shepherd. A crofter further north used to have one, but it was just a puppy,' he said, as Blackie rolled over on to his back. 'Anyway, he's moved away. Perhaps it was something else you saw.'

'It probably *was* something else,' Mandy said dismissively. She was beginning to think that she *had* imagined it. 'What's the library like in the village?' she asked him.

'It's quite good, actually,' Cameron told them. 'I've used it a lot while I've been researching a project about the history of our house for school.'

'Really?' said Mandy.

'I've been doing it on my computer. Tell you what, why don't you both come over and have a look?' Cameron suggested. 'I'll show you around the house too.'

'Thanks,' Mandy replied, picking up the carrier bag, 'but we'd better get this shopping back and then we need to go to the library.' She could see that Cameron was dying to know why they so urgently needed to visit a library, but he was too polite to ask.

'How about tomorrow, then?' he asked. 'The library closes a little bit earlier this afternoon, but you've still got plenty of time. It's down in the village near the church. Nice to meet you both, and you too, Blackie,' he added, patting James's dog before walking away.

When they reached the lodge, Adam Hope was outside, splitting logs from the woodpile for the fire. James grabbed Blackie to stop him getting in the way.

'Hello, you two.' Mr Hope stood up and leaned on the axe. 'You were a long time.'

'We bumped into Cameron,' Mandy told him. 'He's asked us over to the house tomorrow.'

'He's got a computer,' James added.

'Right up your street, James,' Adam Hope said, with a knowing grin.

'We'd like to go back to the village to have a look around, Dad,' Mandy said casually. She didn't want her dad to worry that she was becoming obsessed by wolves.

'Fine,' Adam Hope replied easily. 'Leave the shopping there – I'll put it away.'

'Thanks, Dad,' said Mandy.

When they reached the village, they followed Cameron's instructions and found the library – a red-brick building with a big window on one side. Inside, the librarian was busy working on the computer.

James tied Blackie's lead to a post near the window and they pushed open the door and went inside. It was warm and quiet with children's drawings pinned up around the bookshelves. In one corner there were tables and chairs where you could sit and read. An elderly white-haired man was dozing over a newspaper.

The librarian was young with long blonde hair held back by a headband. She looked up enquiringly. 'Can I help you?' she asked in a soft voice.

'We're visitors here, so we don't have a library card,' Mandy began. 'But we wondered if we could look up some information about wolves?' she finished, looking expectantly at the young woman.

'Well, we have better than that,' the librarian said, smiling broadly at them both. 'We have the real thing in the wildlife park up the road – lovely creatures! I took my little girl to see them last week.' She bent over and rummaged in a drawer. 'Here's a form for you to fill in,' she said.

'You don't mind the wolves living nearby?' Mandy asked, glancing at James and raising her eyebrows in surprise. 'We heard that there was some opposition.'

'Yes, but most of us are in favour of the park. It does very useful work, you know,' she said, sitting up straight again. 'Here we are, just fill in your name and address. I'll show you where to look.'

After a few minutes the librarian, Mandy and James had gathered armfuls of books.

'Phew!' said James, as they piled them on to a table.

'Have fun,' said the librarian, before going back to her desk.

Mandy's heart sank. There were at least ten big thick books. 'We'll be here for ever!' she told James.

'It won't take long to find what we want,' James said encouragingly. 'I'm a bit worried that Blackie might get cold outside, though.'

They glanced out of the window. Blackie was lying down with his head on his paws. As if reading their minds, the librarian came over to them. 'It's not strictly allowed, but if you're going to be in here for a while, you may as well bring your dog in. We don't want it freezing to the ground out there, do we?' she said.

James dashed outside before she could change her mind and collected Blackie. To their surprise, Blackie lay down beside James at once.

He was so quiet that they almost forgot he was there.

'He must know that he'll be sent out into the cold if he's noisy,' James said quietly.

Mandy and James leafed through the books, but couldn't find anything specific enough about wolves that were native to Scotland. Mandy was just beginning to lose hope when James exclaimed loudly, 'Yes! Here it is.'

'The librarian looked over at them and frowned.

'Sorry,' James mouthed back as he pushed the book towards Mandy. 'Look,' he told her. 'Here it is! Everything we need.'

Mandy and James shared the book and began to read. Soon they had discovered that most of Scotland was once covered by great ancient forests that were full of wild animals.

'Look at this,' James whispered to Mandy. 'There used to be bears here too. The last one was killed a thousand years ago.'

'But what about wolves?' Mandy asked. 'When was the last wolf seen?' She turned a page and gave a small gasp. There were several photographs showing the methods used to kill wolves.

'Yuk!' James declared softly, anger in his voice. 'Just imagine being caught in that!' he said, pointing to a picture of a large metal trap. Two rows of sharp-looking, pointed teeth surrounded a flat metal plate. 'They bury it in the ground,' James explained, 'and when something steps on the plate, it triggers the jaws to snap shut!'

Mandy shuddered. She couldn't imagine how terrifying it would be to be caught in such a trap. She imagined it clamping shut with a horrible metal clang. She turned the page quickly.

A heading glared out at her – 'The Last Wild Wolf in Scotland.' With a sinking heart, Mandy began to read.

'Oh no!' she exclaimed and read aloud, ' "The last known wolf in Scotland was shot in 1743." ' Mandy carefully closed the book. 'There couldn't be any left now, could there, James?' she asked, her voice thin with defeat.

James shook his head. 'Not after all this time. I'm sure someone would have seen them,' he said sadly. 'I've found some more facts about wolves, though.' He opened a book and flicked through until he found what he was looking for.

'This book says that wolves are *very* intelligent. Apparently, each wolf's howl is different and wolves can recognise each other's howls from several miles away. They live in family packs, where older wolves look after younger ones and the top wolf – the head of the pack – is called the alpha male. It also says . . .' James paused and looked seriously at Mandy.

'Go on, tell me,' Mandy said glumly. She guessed from James's expression that she wasn't going to like what he had to say.

'Well, it says that wolves are often killed because people are frightened of them, not because they've attacked humans,' James said, shutting the book. 'Wolves seem to be having a pretty rough time everywhere. They're endangered in lots of countries.'

'All the more reason for them to stay at the wildlife park,' Mandy said, her voice rising. 'It's time . . .'

'*Shhhh!*' The white-haired man had woken up and was glaring at them.

'It's time,' Mandy whispered to James, 'that there were a lot more wolves around, *I* think.'

'We'll be closing soon,' the librarian called over to them.

Mandy looked out of the window. It was beginning to get dark. 'We'd better hurry,' she said, piling the books on top of each other. 'We don't want to get lost in the dark.'

They thanked the librarian and set off for the estate.

'Imagine, when this was all forest, there would have been bears and wolves *everywhere*,' Mandy said, spreading her arms wide.

'And lynx and wild cattle and elk,' James added. 'I bet it was a really wild place to be.'

'It's sort of sad, isn't it?' pondered Mandy, as they walked past the main house and turned down the track. 'To think, whole species of animals disappeared from this area before we had a chance to see the animals in the wild.'

'That's why wildlife parks are important,' said James.

Dusk was just falling when they emerged from the wood and saw the lights of the lodge. Mandy realised that they'd missed lunch completely. Porridge *must* be filling.

Later that evening, after a meal of vegetarian chilli and salad, they sat by the fire in the parlour. Blackie lay well out of reach of the sparks.

'I meant to tell you, while I was getting dinner ready I heard a news item about the young wolves at the wildlife park,' Emily Hope said.

Mandy and James sat up quickly.

'What did it say?' Mandy asked urgently. 'I can't believe that I missed it!'

'It's all right, Mandy. I listened very carefully.' Mrs Hope gave her a knowing smile. 'I knew you'd want to hear all about it. Apparently, the wolves are captive-bred juveniles, less than two years old. They're from different packs – the hope is that eventually they will breed.'

'Great,' Mandy said.

'That's the good news, Mandy,' her mum said. 'The bad news is that the local farmers and gamekeepers are campaigning against them.'

'But it's so stupid!' Mandy started to say more, but Emily Hope shook her head.

'They have a right to their point of view, Mandy,' she said. 'They do have their livelihoods to worry about. They're worried that the wolves might escape and start killing their livestock.'

'But we read up about wolves this afternoon. Hundreds of years ago, before people started killing lots of them, wolves used to keep the deer herds under control naturally,' Mandy explained.

'But things were rather different then,' Mrs Hope said. Then she softened. 'I certainly don't agree with the farmers' attitude, though. They want to get rid of them any way they can.'

Mandy was horrified. 'What could they do?' she asked urgently.

'I hope they're not talking about using traps,' Mr Hope said from the depths of an armchair. 'Those contraptions are positively barbaric. And illegal as well!'

Mandy clenched her fists. She could feel anger welling up inside her as she remembered the trap that she'd read about in the library book. She slipped off her shoes, drew her feet up on to the chair and sat hugging her knees. In the background, she could hear her parents and James talking, but she couldn't stop thinking about the young wolves' predicament.

Suddenly she began to feel uncomfortable. It was as if someone was watching her. Glancing around the room, Mandy's gaze was drawn to the window. She felt her body go rigid and held her breath. It was there! The wolf was there! It was staring right at her . . .

This time, it couldn't possibly be her imagination. The wolf was enormous – Mandy could see its great mane of white fur shining in the moonlight. And the wolf's gaze was so intense that it seemed to bore right into her. She stared back at the wolf, not daring to look away for an instant, in case it disappeared.

'Mandy!' She could hear Emily Hope calling to her. Mandy didn't want to move, even to nod her head.

'Dad's suggesting we go to the wildlife park tomorrow,' Mrs Hope said and laughed. 'Would you like to go, or is that a silly question?'

Mandy knew she had to respond. For a brief second she dragged her gaze away from the sad, yellow eyes of the great wolf to nod agreement to her mum.

But when she looked back, the wolf was gone.

Four

'Or would you rather do something else?' Mr Hope was saying, as Mandy refocused on the room. She looked at the expectant faces of her parents and James. They were all waiting for an answer.

'Yes, of course,' Mandy said quickly, trying to keep her voice normal and wondering what on earth they'd been saying.

'Which one? You'd like to visit the wildlife park?' Mr Hope asked, his eyes twinkling. 'Or do something else?'

'The wildlife park, please,' said Mandy, trying desperately to resist the urge to keep glancing at the window.

'Good, then that's settled,' said Adam Hope, standing up and walking across to the dresser. 'Look what I discovered this morning.' He opened the cupboard and pointed to an assortment of board games. 'Who's for a game of Scrabble?'

Mandy tried, but she just couldn't concentrate. She was thinking so hard about the old wolf that she almost jumped out of her skin when her mum clicked her fingers in front of her face.

'What's going on in there, Mandy Hope?' said Mrs Hope, giving her a concerned smile. 'You're not with us tonight, are you?'

'Sorry, Mum,' Mandy said, shrugging her shoulders. 'I can't seem to concentrate.'

'It wouldn't be anything to do with wolves at the window?' Mrs Hope asked, sighing and raising her eyebrows. 'Don't you think that if there *were* wolves roaming the Mudie Estate, someone would have seen them?'

'I know,' Mandy said, nodding her head slowly. 'It's just . . . well, it's nothing really.' She didn't want to worry her parents. Now James was giving her a peculiar look too. 'All right, then,' she said brightly. 'Who's winning?'

But Mandy was too far behind to catch up and James had a spectacular win.

That night, Mandy lay tossing and turning in bed for what seemed like hours.

'Am I *ever* going to get to sleep tonight?' she asked herself, as she tossed and turned for the hundredth time. She lay and listened to the reassuring sounds of the forest. An owl was hooting to its mate and in the distance she heard the sharp bark of a fox. Then, just as she was drifting off to sleep at last, she was startled wide-awake.

Clang!

The ominous clanging sound of metal hitting metal seemed very near. Mandy lay motionless in the bed, frantically trying to work out what it was she'd heard.

Metal hitting metal? Mandy thought to herself, feeling a cold shiver run through her. *A trap! That's what it must have been – a trap snapping shut.* She sat bolt upright in bed and cracked her head on the beam. *They could be out in the forest setting traps right now!* Mandy jumped out of bed and flew to the window. She pushed it open and leaned out as far as she could.

The howl began low and slow. Mandy's scalp prickled and she felt as if her blood had run cold. Gradually, it built up until it was a deafening '*AWOOOOO*' that echoed off the hills. Then, abruptly, the howling stopped. Mandy craned her neck to catch the last echoes as they faded away.

The forest was now silent and still. Mandy was frozen to the spot, her breath steaming in the icy air. There *was* a wolf out there. Surely everyone must have heard the eerie howling?

Mandy stood in her bedroom trying to calm herself down, and wondering what to do next. Her first reaction had been to wake her parents, but something made her hesitate. Why hadn't they – and James – come rushing out to tell *her* about it?

Gradually, she realised how cold she was getting and how tired she was. Perhaps now she would be able to sleep. She reached for the icy handle on the window to pull it shut.

Whooosh!

Suddenly a gust of air rushed past Mandy's ears and something soft touched her hair. She gasped, staggered backwards and then heaved a sigh of relief as she saw an owl swoop away into the darkness. Its silent wings had brushed her head.

Mandy leaned against the window and laughed silently to herself. She really was letting the business with the wolf get to her. She would find out about the clanging noise the next morning, but now she was going back to bed – to sleep!

Suddenly, she heard the scraping sound of her bedroom door opening. Mandy spun round in alarm. 'Who is it?' she hissed. 'James, is that you?'

But there was no answer and still the door continued to move. Now Mandy could hear another sound – *thump, thump, thump!* Clenching her fists defiantly, she took a step forward. 'Who are you?' she said, yanking the door open with all her strength.

Standing in the doorway, tail thumping against the door frame, was Blackie.

'Blackie!' Mandy cried out with relief. 'What are you trying to do? You almost frightened the life out of me!'

She switched on the light and looked around the room. Everything seemed perfectly normal.

'What's the matter with me, Blackie?' She grinned as she bent down to rub his head. 'First I get spooked by a toad, then a clanging noise, then a wolf, then an owl – and now a dog!'

Blackie just seemed to grin back at her as he rolled over and thumped his tail on the floor.

Mandy could see light coming from James's room. Blackie must have pushed open the door and sneaked out. She tapped softly on the door and went in to find James deeply engrossed in a computer magazine.

'Blackie's just pretended to be a ghost,' she told James.

'He does things like that in the night,' James laughed. 'He must've done it to make you jump.'

'He did!' she agreed. 'Especially coming right after that clanging noise and the howling.'

'Howling?' James said in a puzzled voice. 'Clanging?' he wrinkled up his nose. 'I don't know what you're talking about.'

'You were awake,' Mandy said, staring at him in amazement. 'You *must* have heard it.'

'It's been as quiet as anything tonight,' James said, closing his magazine. 'I did hear an owl and I thought I heard a fox bark, but I couldn't be sure.'

'But there was a clanging noise, like the jaws of a trap closing,' Mandy said desperately. 'Then I heard a wolf howling – a really sad, lonely howl. It sounded like it was coming from the forest. How did you miss it? It went on for *ages*!'

'Nope! Didn't hear any of that,' James said, shaking his head. He looked at his watch. 'It is quite late. Are you sure you didn't dream it?'

'Of course I didn't,' Mandy said indignantly. 'How could I have dreamed it when I was wide awake? You were more likely to fall asleep reading that boring magazine.' She scratched Blackie's head. 'I mean, you didn't even notice that Blackie had gone.'

'That's true,' James agreed.

But, safely back in bed, Mandy knew that James could not possibly have missed the wolf's howling. She'd heard it. So why hadn't he? She was still puzzling over this when she eventually fell asleep.

Bonnng!

Mandy woke with a start. Not *more* loud clanging noises!

'Breakfast is served,' her dad called up the stairs in a snooty voice, trying to sound like an old-fashioned butler. 'And if you're not up in five minutes, I'll come upstairs and bang this gong again!'

She looked at her watch. She'd overslept. She felt as if she still needed at least two more hours' sleep, but remembered that they were going to the wildlife park today. Filled with energy and enthusiasm at the thought of seeing the two young wolves, she sprang out of bed, dressed quickly and ran downstairs.

Her dad was standing in the hall, with the gong ready for action. Mandy put her hands over her ears as Mr Hope hit it firmly with a leather-covered mallet.

'I've always wanted to do that,' Adam Hope said in a satisfied voice. 'These were used to call people to meals in the olden days.'

'Was that when you were a boy, Dad?' Mandy asked with a cheeky grin, ducking out of the way and dodging into the kitchen. 'Where's James?' she asked her mum.

As if in answer to her question, James and Blackie burst in through the back door. Blackie's lead was trailing behind him and James looked exhausted. 'Blackie . . . walk . . .' he panted, and flopped into a chair. Within seconds, he was joined by everyone else. Soon they were all enjoying plates of fluffy scrambled eggs and toast, washed down with mugs of tea.

'We can go to the wildlife park directly after breakfast,' Mrs Hope said, reaching for the teapot. 'That will give us lots of time. We could even have lunch there. More toast, James?'

'Thanks,' James said, taking a slice. 'I can't wait to see the wolves. I wonder how big they'll be?'

'A fair size, I'd imagine. They won't be little cubs any more,' Adam Hope said. 'Nowhere near as heavy as an adult though – *they* can weigh up to forty kilos.'

Mandy looked thoughtful. 'I wonder how close we'll be able to get to them?' she said.

'We'll soon find out,' Emily Hope said, with a smile. 'It won't take long to get there. And if we're all finished,' she said, beginning to clear the table, 'we can make a move.'

James looked sternly at Blackie, who had jumped up and made for the door. 'I'm afraid you've got to stay behind,' he told him. 'Dogs aren't allowed in the wildlife park. But we'll take you out for a long walk when we get back, I promise.'

'I'm going to do some cooking this afternoon,' Adam Hope told them as he started the engine of the Animal Ark Land-rover. 'There's a wonderful old cookbook in the dresser drawer. It's got a recipe for neeps and tatties. That's turnips and potatoes to you two.'

'Sounds good,' James said, doing up his seat belt.

Though the wildlife park had been set up on land belonging to the Mudie Estate, the entrance was a few miles away. They drove out of the estate and along narrow winding lanes, following signs for 'Mudie Wildlife Park'. Mr Hope turned up the drive, and drove through an ivy-covered stone entrance and past a group of old buildings, before following a sign to the carpark. As they got out of the Land-rover, a tall man with a shock of white hair came striding towards them.

'Welcome,' he called to them, holding out his hand in greeting to Adam and Emily. 'You must be Angus's veterinarian friends. It's good to meet you. I'm Duncan Marriott and I run this place.' He had deep-blue eyes that crinkled up when he smiled. He was wearing khaki trousers and a thick sweater in deep forest green. 'Mudie

Wildlife Park' was embroidered neatly in red on the top pocket.

'And you must be Mandy and James,' he said, shaking hands with them both. 'Angus tells me that you're as keen on animals as I am. That takes some doing!'

Mandy knew immediately that she was going to like this man.

'How did you know who we were?' Mr Hope said, looking faintly surprised.

'You advertise yourself,' Duncan said, pointing to the Animal Ark motif on the Land-rover's door. 'Come and meet my wife, Sally. If you like, we'll take you around the park ourselves!'

'That's very kind of you,' Emily Hope said. 'But we don't want to disturb you if you're busy.'

'No, no,' Duncan said, smiling at them. 'I always check the park thoroughly every morning. It'll be nice to have some company.'

'We might be able to get really close to the animals,' Mandy whispered to James as they followed Duncan into his office.

'Angus's friends have arrived,' Duncan said to a woman sitting behind a desk. 'Here's Sally, she handles most of the paperwork and keeps this place running,' he told them.

Sally stood up and came out from behind the desk. 'I'm very pleased to meet you,' she said, when Emily Hope had introduced them all. Sally had a soft lilting voice, long blonde hair tied back in a ponytail and a smile as friendly as her husband's.

'I'm taking them around,' Duncan told her. 'Have you got time to join us?' He turned to the Hopes and James. 'As well as the office work, Sally is responsible for the gift shop and supervises the restaurant. She also takes care of any young or sick animals.'

'You must be busy!' exclaimed Adam Hope.

'It keeps me on my toes,' laughed Sally. 'My favourite job at the moment is rearing our two new arrivals.'

Mandy felt a tingle of excitement. 'The wolves?' she asked Sally.

'Yes,' she replied, smiling. 'They are absolutely gorgeous – wait until you see them. And they're *so* intelligent, too.'

'It must be hard work, all this,' Emily Hope said, indicating the park with her arm.

'It is,' Sally agreed. 'But at least we have some more keepers now. Before that we were mucking out the animals as well! Let's go!' she said, fetching her coat. 'I can spare some time – we don't get so many visitors in winter.'

Mandy and James walked beside Sally, while Mandy's parents followed behind with Duncan. They all listening avidly as he explained the workings of a wildlife park. Sally stopped at a large wooden building, took out a bunch of keys, and unlocked the door.

'Once a week the animals get a treat,' she told Mandy and James. 'Would you like to come and help me?'

They followed her inside. The walls were lined with shelves stacked with old newspapers, buckets, brooms and brushes. Shovels and rolls of fencing were propped against the walls. In the corner, there was a wheelbarrow full of loaves of bread and cakes.

'Here we are,' Sally said handing them the wrapped loaves. 'Donald at the mini-market lets us have everything from the bakery that hasn't sold.'

Loaded up with loaves and cakes, Mandy and James followed Sally and Duncan to the first enclosure. They stopped in front of a sturdy wooden barrier with a deep ditch on the other side. In the middle of the enclosure was a large rocky area surrounded by woodland. 'This is where Dolly lives,' Duncan said, leaning on the fence. Mandy peered around the field but could see no animals at all.

'Rustle the bags,' Duncan told them.

Mandy and James shook the paper bags that contained the cakes. Within seconds a big brown bear appeared from among the boulders. She loped over to them and then stood up on her back legs and pawed the air with her arms.

'Mandy and James – meet Dolly,' Sally said gently. 'Dolly came here from Eastern Europe. Street vendors had been making money out of her. They'd been parading her around and tormenting her to make her dance. She's really gentle now, but when we first got her, she'd been so badly treated that she was terrified and lashed out at everyone.' Sally took a doughnut from Mandy's bag. 'Throw her this,' she said, handing it to Mandy.

Mandy threw the cake and Dolly caught it in her mouth. 'Oh no!' Mandy cried out. 'Look, James! She's got a hole through her nose.'

'Animals have very sensitive noses and they'd put a ring through hers to control her,' Duncan explained. 'She must have had the odd treat though, because she certainly loves these cakes!'

Dolly looked expectantly at Mandy, but Duncan and Sally were already moving on. 'I'm sorry. No more,' Mandy told the bear softly as she and James reluctantly followed them.

'There were bears in Scotland many years ago,' Duncan said, his voice wistful. 'But they were wiped out by hunters. The same thing happened to the wolves.'

On the far side of the next field, they could

see a herd of animals grazing on straw. Their heads sprang up when they saw the party.

'Reindeer,' Sally explained, as they trotted over to the fence. She ripped open a loaf of bread and handed slices to Mandy and James for them to throw in. 'They're from Sweden. Can you guess the name of that big male?'

'Rudolph?' Mandy asked, and laughed when Sally nodded.

'Eventually, our aim is to breed in captivity all species of animal that once lived in Scotland,' Duncan said as they moved off again. 'Then people can appreciate how much we've lost.'

Twenty minutes later they had fed the Shetland ponies and the wild boar, before stopping at an enclosure containing a pair of pine martens.

'Weren't these almost wiped out?' Adam Hope asked Duncan.

'That's right. They were once on the edge of extinction, mainly because of gin-traps.' Duncan answered. 'It was good conservation work that saved them; that and banning traps.'

'We heard some people complaining about the wolves yesterday,' Mandy said, her face full of concern.

'Some of them were really angry,' James added.

Duncan put his hands on his hips and stared into the distance. 'I know, but they really don't need to be worried. The wolves can't escape,' he said, with a pained expression. 'They've settled in well. But, like a lot of young animals, they're frisky and full of energy. They're bound to be seen charging around the enclosure and that can give the public the wrong impression.'

'It doesn't necessarily mean that they're trying to get out,' Mr Hope agreed.

'True,' Duncan grinned. 'Come on, let's introduce you.' And he set off towards the farthest end of the park.

'Their enclosure is quite big,' said Sally as they walked alongside a tall, solid-looking chain-link fence, at least a hundred metres long. 'We wanted it to be as similar to the wolves' natural habitat as possible.'

'Will you release the wolves when they're older?' James asked. 'That's what some people seemed worried about.'

Duncan laughed. 'I don't think that's even remotely possible at the moment. There's far too much opposition. And it's something that would need very careful thought and planning, not to be undertaken lightly.'

'So they're safe in here?' Mandy asked.

'Definitely. All of the enclosures back on to the high perimeter fence,' Duncan explained. 'It's made up of two layers of chain link with a gap between. The outer fence has barbed wire on the top, to make it even more secure.'

'To keep the animals in?' James asked.

'And to keep people out!' said Sally. 'There's also a ditch inside the perimeter fence, so that if it snows heavily and piles up, the animals can't climb out.'

'You've thought of everything!' Adam Hope commented. 'I'm impressed.'

'This inner fence is strong too,' Duncan said, pushing hard at the fence to prove it. 'It's buried very deep in the ground, so it's virtually impossible to dig underneath it. And just to keep people happy we're going to make the fence even higher.'

Sally put her hand on Mandy's shoulder. 'Look Mandy,' she said in a voice full of excitement. 'There they are. What do you think of them?'

Five

Mandy stared through the wire mesh. Bounding towards her were two of the most gorgeous creatures that she had ever seen. The wolves stopped close to the fence and looked at the little party quizzically.

One had a glossy dark-brown coat and a black face with a pink spot on his nose. The other was biscuit-coloured with a gold stripe on its nose and gold-tipped ears.

'They look like big German shepherd puppies, but their coats are so thick and long,' Mandy said in an awed voice. 'Do they let you stroke them?' she asked Sally.

Sally nodded. 'At the moment they think I'm their mum. They're not big enough yet to be able to fend for themselves completely. Would you like to meet them?'

'Meet them?' Mandy repeated, looking up at her parents.

'You mean – go inside the enclosure?' added James.

Adam Hope grinned. 'We weren't expecting this, were we?' he said, as Mandy and James looked back in amazement.

Duncan unlocked the outer gate and they filed through into a safety cage with a gate at the other side. Sally waited for Duncan to lock the outer gate, before undoing the inner one. 'Let me go first to settle them,' she said softly.

The young wolves ran to Sally and rubbed their bodies against her legs. Then she beckoned to Mandy.

Mandy felt excitement tingle through her body as, with Duncan beside her, she walked towards the wolves. They stared at her, eyes wide with curiosity, then trotted over. She bent down slowly and began to stroke their thick coats.

'You *are* wonderful!' she said, running her hand down the dark wolf's back and along its

bushy tail. 'What big feet you have.' Not to be left out, the gold wolf nudged at her knees, trying to push the dark wolf out of the way. One by one, James and her parents came across – soon they were all making a fuss of the young wolves.

'As they get older, they'll have to lose this contact with humans. They'll need their wolf instinct if they are ever to form a pack.'

Mrs Hope looked at her watch. 'I think we've kept these kind people from their work long enough. Why don't we go and have some lunch?' she suggested.

'Can we catch you up?' Mandy pleaded as they left the enclosure. 'I'm not hungry, and there's so much more to see!'

'You're never hungry when there are animals to be seen, Mandy,' Adam Hope said. 'But what about you, James?'

'Yes, I'm starving,' James burst out. Then, seeing the disappointment on Mandy's face, backtracked. 'No, actually, I don't think I'm *really* hungry, not yet,' he said, his face turning pink as everyone laughed.

'Why don't you go and see the Soay sheep, Mandy?' Sally suggested, after Mrs Hope had nodded her approval. 'And the Highland cattle are worth a look too.'

Mandy glanced back at the wolves. They were bouncing around each other like overgrown puppies, chasing each other's tail.

'I wonder if we'll get a chance to come back and see them again before we go home?' Mandy said, setting off around the park. 'Aren't they gorgeous?'

'I thought they'd look alike,' said James, falling into step with Mandy. 'I didn't realise there was such variety in the colours and patterns of their coats.'

They found the Highland cattle, with their long, shaggy coats and enormous horns. Then they visited the brown-fleeced Soay sheep. The information plaque said that these were the only really wild sheep in Scotland. They were lovely, but Mandy couldn't tear her thoughts away from the wolves.

'You can imagine how big and powerful they'll be when they're fully grown, can't you?' she said to James, as they made their way back to the restaurant.

'Wow, you're not kidding,' James agreed. 'They wouldn't want to play with you then.

They'd be too busy hunting.'

Mandy and James arrived at the restaurant just as everyone's lunch was served. Luckily for James, Mrs Hope hadn't forgotten them and he eagerly tucked into his pizza.

By the time they'd said goodbye to the Marriotts and driven back to the lodge, it was mid-afternoon.

'Come on, James,' Mandy said, as she jumped out of the Land-rover. 'We promised Blackie that we'd take him for a walk.'

'Wait a minute,' James called after her. 'Look who's coming down the track.'

Mandy turned to see Cameron sprinting down the track from the main house with Beattie at his heels.

'Hello,' he said, puffing slightly. 'I saw you drive in and thought I'd catch you. Would you like to come and see the house and my project this afternoon? You could stay for tea as well, if you like.'

Mandy looked at her parents. 'Is that OK, Mum?' she asked.

'Of course! It's very nice of you to invite them, Cameron,' Mrs Hope said. 'But they *must* take Blackie out for a long walk first. He's been shut up since this morning.'

'That's fine with me. Beattie and I will come along too,' Cameron said. He looked down at Beattie, who was wiggling her body and wagging her tail with excitement, and grinned. 'But I can't guarantee that she'll keep up with Blackie!'

'We don't mind,' Mandy said, bending down and stroking the little chocolate-coloured dog. 'She's *so* sweet.'

James freed Blackie from the house and they set off into the woods. After being shut in for so long, Blackie was full of energy – darting all over the place, sniffing scents and chasing falling leaves. Beattie ran from one side of the path to the other, trying to keep up with him on her short legs.

'Blackie's given her a new lease of life,' Cameron said. 'She hasn't been this active in months.'

'Mum and Dad sometimes tell people with old dogs that a puppy might help to liven them up,' Mandy said.

'Maybe you should get Beattie a friend,' James suggested.

'Perhaps I will,' Cameron agreed.

They were busy talking about dogs and

puppies and about life at Animal Ark when James stopped suddenly. 'Where are we now? I can't hear the dogs moving about.'

Cameron stopped and looked around. 'We've come quite a long way. This is where the estate borders the wildlife park. Beattie!' he called, loud and clear.

They stood still and listened for a sound. Nothing.

'Blackie, here boy! Come on!' James shouted.

Mandy put her hand up to silence him. 'I can hear noises over there,' she said, pointing over to the right.

As they watched, Blackie came into view among the distant trees. 'See,' James said proudly. 'He's quite obedient, really.'

Mandy and Cameron looked at each other and both burst out laughing.

'You wish, James,' Mandy said, grinning broadly.

As James agreed in a good-natured way, Blackie began barking. Then, suddenly, the sound was cut off by a terrible clanging noise. Mandy recognised it immediately as the same sound that she had heard last night. Metal hitting metal. She felt light-headed and faint and shook her head to clear the sensation.

'What was that?' James and Cameron said together.

But, before Mandy could answer, they heard a dreadful scream and howl of pain. She knew for certain that it wasn't a wolf. It was Blackie.

Mandy saw the blood drain out of James's face as he dashed off towards Blackie.

Mandy raced after James. *Please don't let Blackie be hurt*, she said to herself. *Please!*

She could feel Cameron running close behind her. He must be just as worried about Beattie, she thought. They hurtled up and over a small hummock and there, huddled trembling in a ditch and licking his paw, was Blackie. Standing guard beside him, wide-eyed and shivering with fright, was Beattie.

'Blackie!' James cried in a worried voice. Slipping and slithering, he scrambled down into the ditch and buried his face in his dog's neck. Cameron clambered down and scooped his little dog up. Mandy watched James and Blackie, her vision blurred with tears. She half fell into the ditch and quickly helped to examine Blackie's paw.

'James?' she said, urgently, nudging his arm.

'James, I'm sure it's not too bad.'

James lifted an anxious face. 'I know, Mandy. It's just that I was so scared,' he said in a voice thick with relief. 'I couldn't bear it if anything happened to him.'

Blackie had had enough of being hugged to death and was struggling to get up. But every time he tried, he yelped in pain.

'Look James,' Mandy said, gently running her hand down the dog's foreleg. 'See, his leg's bleeding.' Blackie gave a soft yelp, and looked at Mandy with reproachful eyes. 'Don't worry, Blackie,' she said. 'We'll carry you back to the lodge.'

'He's had a close shave you know,' Cameron said, his voice sombre. 'Look here.'

There, hidden in the grass and staked to the ground, was a metal trap. Its vicious teeth were clenched together.

'Blackie could have lost a leg in that, or worse!' Cameron said angrily. 'Gamekeepers once used them. It's virtually impossible for a creature to escape,' he said, nodding towards it. 'But it has been known for an animal to chew its own leg off.'

Mandy shuddered. 'We need to get Blackie

back to Mum and Dad, so that they can treat him,' she said, beginning to feel fury at whoever had set the trap. They must have known what injuries they could cause.

'I'll wait here,' Cameron said, sitting down with Beattie on his lap. 'Could you call the police and tell PC Farish what's happened? These traps are illegal. My dad will need to know about it too, as it's been set on his land.'

James took off his coat and made a sling for them to carry Blackie home.

'Be careful where you tread, now,' Cameron warned them. 'Whoever set that trap could have set others.'

As they carried Blackie home, Mandy began to realise something.

'James, do you remember that noise I heard last night?' she said urgently. 'Don't you see what this means? It *was* real after all. I didn't dream it or imagine it. Someone *was* out there setting traps and I *heard* them!'

James paused for a second and glanced up from watching where he was treading. 'What about the howl? There wasn't a wolf caught, was there?' he said, in a careful voice.

'There *is* a wolf, James,' Mandy's voice was

positive. 'I can't prove it yet, but I will.'

They emerged from the trees in front of the lodge, where they could see Mandy's dad getting something out of the Land-rover.

'Dad!' Mandy shouted at the top of her voice. She could see him looking frantically around. 'Over here,' she yelled.

Adam Hope ran up to them. 'What's wrong? What's happened to Blackie? Here, give him to me,' Mr Hope said briskly. He carefully took the coat with Blackie inside from James. Mandy ran alongside, explaining all about the traps.

'And will you phone PC Farish and Cameron's dad, please?' she asked her dad as they arrived at the lodge. Emily Hope had come out to see what was happening and met the party at the door.

'You deal with Blackie, love. I'll go and phone Angus,' Mr Hope said, putting James's dog down carefully on the rug in the kitchen.

'Could you run into our bedroom for me, Mandy?' asked Mrs Hope, but Mandy was already on her way. She ran back into the kitchen with the big, black, leather bag. Her dad was on the phone in the hall.

'Apparently, Angus. No, Cameron is fine –

he's waiting by the trap. You'll call the police?' He hesitated and listened. 'Fine, then Mandy can lead us back to him. We'll wait for you here.'

'Fortunately, the wound is superficial. But his paw is badly bruised and sprained,' Mrs Hope was saying. 'I'll strap it up so that it's not so painful, but he'll need to keep off it for a while. He's got an injury of the carpal joint,' she told her husband. 'He must've just nicked his leg in the trap and sprained it as he fell.'

'From the sound of things, Blackie was lucky,' Mr Hope said, rocking backwards and forwards on his heels. 'What sort of a person sets a steel trap in a private woodland, where animals and children run about? It's completely beyond me!'

He walked over to the window and looked out while Mandy helped Mrs Hope strap up Blackie's paw. 'Here's the police car now. Angus is in it too,' Mr Hope said. 'James, why don't you stay with Blackie? I'll go with Mandy to find Cameron.'

'Thanks,' James said gratefully. 'I would like to stay with him to help keep him calm.'

'He'd better sleep down here, tonight,' Mrs Hope said, getting up from the floor. 'I'll go and get his bed from upstairs.'

Mandy and her dad went outside to meet Angus and the police officer.

Angus introduced them and PC Farish shook hands with them both. He was tall and thin with very short blond hair. In one hand he held a large, brown, leather bag.

'This is a very bad do,' said the police officer. 'I have four dogs of my own at home. The thought of one of them being caught in a trap . . .' he said, smacking his fist into the palm of his other hand. 'Lead the way to where you left Cameron, young lady. The sooner we reach him the better,' he said, glancing at Angus and Adam.

Mandy guessed that they were worried that the person who set the trap might come back to finish off any poor animal unlucky enough to be caught. Mandy hurried through the woods as fast as she could.

Cameron was sitting with his back against a tree with Beattie asleep in his arms. Adam Hope gently took the little dog and Angus helped his son get up.

'Ugh, I'm stiff. I didn't want to move for fear of waking her,' Cameron said, stretching his arms above his head. 'She's too old to have shocks like this.'

PC Farish was on his hands and knees beside the trap, prising the stakes out of the ground with a claw hammer. Mandy bent down to look. It sent a shiver through her.

'It's evil!' the police officer growled, without looking up. 'They hammer these so deep into the ground because they know that an injured animal will have the strength of desperation. They can't risk the animal pulling the trap out of the ground and walking off with it attached to its limb.'

'What I can't understand is, what are they after?' Angus asked the policeman. 'There are no deer in this part of the estate and I can't believe that anyone around here would go to such trouble for a few rabbits. It's a mystery to me.'

PC Farish had the trap free now and he zipped it firmly into the leather bag. 'I'll make sure that there's a photo of this in the local paper, warning people to watch out,' he said. 'And I would suggest that you take great care when you're out with the dogs until we've caught whoever is responsible.'

The light was fading when they got back to the lodge. It had been a hectic afternoon and they'd all had a fright. Mandy wasn't sorry when Cameron suggested that they visit his house the following morning instead of that evening. But, after supper, she couldn't settle.

Noticing her restlessness, Mr Hope said, 'If you want a job, Mandy, you can fill the log basket. We're down to our last one.' He dropped a log on to the fire.

'Right,' said Mandy, springing up and grabbing the basket.

'I'll help you,' James said quickly.

In the hall they grabbed their coats, opened the front door and stepped outside.

'What do you think is going on in the woods?' James asked, looking at her seriously.

Mandy began loading the basket. 'I don't know,' she replied.

'But you must have *some* ideas,' James persisted. 'I know when you've got something on your mind, and tonight, you *definitely* have. I'm sure your mum and dad have noticed it too.'

Mandy glanced up at James and said slowly, 'I've been thinking about it a lot and I can't come up with anything concrete, but . . .' She paused and stood up, frowning and staring at the trees.

'But?' James prompted.

Mandy turned and looked him in the eye. 'I know you don't believe me, but something tells me that it's all to do with the young wolves – the old wolf, the noises I'm hearing, the trap, everything. It doesn't make much sense, but it's what I believe.'

'Mandy, look!' James grabbed her arm. 'There's something moving in the woods.'

'Where?' She strained to see.

James pointed up the path. 'There! In that patch of moonlight, beside that big oak tree! See, it's creeping away.'

Mandy made an instant decision. 'I'm going to follow it,' she said, zipping up her coat. 'It could be someone laying more traps. Get Dad!'

'Mandy!' James yelled in protest.

But she was off as fast as her feet would carry her. At the oak tree, she left the path and followed the shape into the wood. She could just make out movement ahead, but it wasn't very clear. She'd have to get closer. A cloud drifted slowly across the bright face of the moon and the forest became so dark that she could hardly see a thing. *I wish I'd brought a torch*, she thought.

There was something moving up ahead, silhouetted against the sky. Whatever it was moved deeper and deeper into the forest. She knew that she had no choice – she must follow it or lose it. She sent out a silent message; *Hurry, Dad. Please!*

Suddenly PC Farish's words came back to her. '*Take great care . . .*'

Mandy's heart was in her mouth as she continued walking forward. Before she took each step, she paused with bated breath, for fear of stepping into a trap. The moon came out again and with shock she saw that the dark shape was motionless, almost directly ahead of her. Mandy couldn't make out what it was. She stood very still and waited for it to move on.

To her horror it turned and began to walk towards her. And then, with a sick feeling in her stomach, Mandy realised it had been a trick. She had been lured deep into the forest – now the thing was coming back for her.

As the creature drew closer, Mandy could make out a shimmering haze all around. Her eyes widened and she gasped in recognition. It was a wolf. A huge grey wolf.

Mandy half turned, and tried to run, but her

legs felt as heavy as lead and she couldn't move them. Now she could clearly see a dark T-shaped stripe on the animal's face. It was the wolf she had seen at the window. It padded silently closer.

Then, when it was so near enough to touch, it stopped. Its sad, yellow eyes bored into hers.

Mandy tried desperately to speak, but she couldn't make a sound.

Six

The old wolf stared at Mandy with its amazingly yellow eyes. He was enormous, with great, powerful jaws, but Mandy didn't feel afraid. She stared back.

In the distance she heard a cry. 'Mandy!' It was her dad's anxious voice. 'Mandy, where are you?'

Then she heard James's voice, getting closer: 'Mandy, can you hear me?'

Without moving its head, the wolf shifted its gaze to a point behind Mandy. It gave her one last piercing look before turning and padding away. Then the wolf melted into the darkness among the trees – and was gone.

Mandy felt drained, as if her body was about to crumple and collapse. She turned and saw James standing among the trees behind her, staring wide-eyed with amazement.

'You saw it James, didn't you?' Mandy called urgently. She could hear her dad calling again.

James nodded. 'I didn't believe you,' he said earnestly. 'But I saw it standing there, as large as life.'

'Don't say anything yet,' Mandy warned, as Mr Hope came running up. 'Not till we know what it's all about.'

'Are you all right, Mandy?' Adam Hope gasped as he reached her. Even in the gloom, Mandy could see that his face was very pale and his eyes were dark with worry. 'What on earth were you thinking of?' he asked, putting his hands on her shoulders. 'You had us really worried. Mum was all for phoning the police.'

'I thought it was the person who set the traps, Dad,' she said apologetically. 'Once I got into the forest I couldn't see anything. I'm sorry.'

Adam Hope was silent as they left the wood, but once they arrived back at the lodge he looked at them both keenly.

'Now, look here,' he said, his voice serious. 'We've already had one potentially nasty accident today.' He glanced up as Emily Hope came out into the hall. 'Your mum will agree, James gave us a terrible shock saying you were following a figure into the wood. People who set traps like that are *not* playing games. You might have found yourself in all sorts of trouble.'

'But, Dad—' Mandy began.

'No, Mandy, no arguments. I want a promise from both of you that you will stay out of the woods,' Mr Hope demanded, looking from one to the other. 'I mean it. Leave crime-solving to the professionals. Let PC Farish sort it out.'

Mandy looked at her parents' faces. She could tell that they were upset and felt guilty that she was the cause.

'This is supposed to be a relaxing break, Mandy,' her mum added reproachfully. 'We don't want to have to worry about you two every time you leave the lodge.'

'OK, you've got it,' said Mandy glumly. 'I'm sorry. I know I shouldn't have dashed off like that.'

'And me,' said James. 'I'm sorry I scared you too.'

'Then we'll say no more about it,' Mrs Hope told them. 'There's just one more thing, though,' she added.

Mandy looked up at her mum with a worried expression. 'What is it?'

'The little matter of the logs . . .' Her mum pointed out, giving her a broad smile.

'Oh, I'd forgotten all about them,' Mandy said, heading for the door with James hot on her heels.

'What now?' James asked, as soon as they were outside. 'What do we do now?'

Mandy's face was set in a frown. 'We wait and see what happens next,' she sighed. For the second time that evening, she heaved logs into the basket.

'But we can't go in the woods,' James said uneasily. 'We promised.'

'I know, and we may not have to,' she said looking him in the eye. 'Don't forget, the wolf has come to the window twice already.'

Together, they carried the log-filled basket back inside and both sat where they had a clear view of the windows. But by bedtime, they hadn't seen a thing.

*   *   *

Mandy woke early the next morning. It was still dark but she could hear James moving about in his room. His door opened and she heard him run downstairs. She smiled to herself. He'd be anxious to check on Blackie. Soon the tempting smell of bread toasting drifted up the stairs and Mandy guessed that her dad was up. She dressed and went downstairs.

'Morning, love,' Adam Hope greeted her. 'One round of toast coming shortly.'

'Morning, Dad,' she replied. 'Where's James?'

'Blackie's foot is much better this morning,' Mr Hope told her, smiling. 'James has taken him out for a short, gentle stroll.'

'Blackie!' Mandy exclaimed. 'Strolling gently? That'll be the day.'

'I'm afraid that we all – even strong-willed dogs like Blackie – have to bow down to circumstances sometimes!' Mr Hope said pointedly, giving her a meaningful look.

'It's OK, Dad,' Mandy agreed cheerfully. 'I promise we'll be good.'

'I know you will, love,' Mr Hope gave her a grin. 'Don't frighten us like that again, though. I ran so fast, I could have made the Olympic team.'

James came in the kitchen door. 'Look, Mandy,' he said. 'Blackie can almost walk properly.'

'Don't let him overdo it, James,' Mr Hope said. 'He ought to rest it as much as he can.'

'He'd better stay here while we go to Cameron's house, then,' Mandy suggested, helping herself to orange juice.

Adam Hope picked up a tray laden with tea and toast. 'As a special treat, mum's having breakfast in bed today,' he said, as he carried it out of the room. 'She's resting before the party!'

After breakfast, they grabbed their coats and set off for the big house. Climbing the steps to the great oak door, Mandy reached for the huge brass doorknocker.

'James!' she gasped, recoiling in shock. 'Look!'

'Oh, wow!' James said, following Mandy's gaze. 'That's impressive.' The doorknocker was moulded into the shape of a wolf's head, with yellow stones for eyes.

'But why?' Mandy was puzzled. 'Why a wolf's head?'

'Maybe Cameron can tell us,' James shrugged,

lifting the knocker and rapping on the door.

Cameron came to the door. 'Hello, come in! How's Blackie this morning?' he greeted them anxiously.

'He's much better,' James told him, 'but Mr Hope says he's still got to rest.'

'Phew!' said Cameron. 'I've been really worried about him. Beattie was so frightened that she wouldn't go outside the house last night. But she's perked up today, which is a relief.'

Mandy looked around. They were standing in a tall hall, in front of a huge pair of wooden doors. These were covered with intricate carvings of animals. On one side of the doors, a winding staircase led up into darkness.

Cameron flung open the doors and took them inside.

'This is the Great Hall,' he told them. 'The party will be held here tonight.'

Mandy and James stared round the vast room. Logs were burning in the grate of a huge stone fireplace. A colourful coat of arms hung above it. A big basket of pine cones stood nearby. 'We'll put them on the fire later on – they smell really nice,' Cameron added.

Down the centre of the room, long tables were covered with white cloths. 'The caterers will be here after lunch to prepare the food,' Cameron told them, as they walked through the room towards a wide staircase at the end. 'My parents have gone to the station to collect some friends from London,' he said.

'What a wonderful house to live in!' enthused Mandy.

'Well, we only live in a small part of it,' said Cameron. 'It would cost too much to heat the whole building all of the time.'

'What's upstairs?' James asked, looking up the staircase.

'Come and see,' replied Cameron, taking the stairs two at a time.

Soon they were looking down on the Great Hall from high above. 'This,' he said, holding his arms wide apart, 'is the Minstrels' Gallery. This is where musicians used to play years ago. Tonight, we'll have a live band up here.'

'Wow, it's going to be fantastic,' sighed James, walking along the gallery. 'What are all these rooms for?' he added.

'We usually let this area out for holiday-makers,' Cameron explained. 'But tonight it'll be full of family and friends.'

'How many people are you expecting?' asked Mandy.

'We don't know for sure,' Cameron answered her, raising his eyebrows and grinning. 'My dad really loves a party, so Mum always asks lots of people from the village. We never know who's going to turn up!'

He led them back downstairs and opened the door into the Mudies' living quarters. 'We live in the rooms at the back of the house – they're easier to keep warm,' he said, bending down to scoop up an excited Beattie. 'I'm glad Blackie's foot is going to be all right.'

'So am I,' James agreed, making a fuss of the little dog.

Mandy stroked Beattie's head and looked around. These smaller rooms looked much cosier than some other parts of the house. One wall of the sitting-room was almost covered by photos and another was lined from floor to ceiling with books.

'Some of these books look really old,' James said, and Mandy could tell that he was itching to look at them.

'Help yourself,' Cameron offered, putting

Beattie on the floor. 'Just be a little careful with some of the older ones.' Soon, James was poring over the books while Mandy studied the photos on the wall.

'These are some of my ancestors,' Cameron said proudly. 'Mudies have lived in the house for over three hundred years.' He came over and stood next to Mandy. 'If you like animals, you'll love the sketchbook.'

'What sketchbook?' she asked.

Cameron grinned mysteriously. 'It's a very, very, old sketchbook – a family heirloom. I'll show it to you.' He fetched a stool, climbed up and stretched up to the top shelf, scrambling down seconds later with a silver cardboard box.

'Here,' he passed the box to Mandy. 'Have a look, but please be very careful. It's really old and quite fragile.'

She put the box on the table and removed the lid. Inside, wrapped in black tissue paper was a loose-leaved book with a dark green cover. The pages were bound together with thin green ribbon. The book certainly looked very old. Gingerly Mandy lifted it out and turned to the first page, which was all mottled and yellow with age. But, there in the middle of the ancient paper, was a line drawing of a robin. 'It's beautiful,' she breathed. 'James, come and look.'

James put down his book and came over to the table. 'It's good, isn't it?' he agreed. 'It must have been drawn with pen and ink.'

Cameron nodded. 'We think that they might have been painted with watercolors, but all the colours have faded away over the years,' he said.

Mandy turned the page. A portrait of a fox stared out at them.

The next few pictures were of badgers, hedgehogs and owls. But the next picture was much more elaborate than the rest – it was of a young girl sitting in a woodland glade, surarounded by animals. What caught Mandy's eye was a large dog, curled up at her feet, partly hidden by her long dress.

'Is that her dog?' Mandy called to Cameron, who was in the kitchen making drinks.

'There aren't any dogs in the sketchbook,' he called back. 'They're all *wild* animals. That's what made Fiona so special.'

'How do you mean?' Mandy asked, full of curiosity.

Cameron came back into the room with mugs

of hot chocolate and a bowl of crisps. 'Fiona had a way with wild animals. They used to gather round her every time she went into the woods. She used to play with them as if they were pets.'

Mandy looked more closely at the drawing and saw that birds were perched on the girl's hand and a squirrel nestled on her shoulder.

'But what about this dog?' Mandy persisted, pointing at the picture.

'That's not a dog,' Cameron laughed. 'That's a wolf!'

Mandy looked across at James, startled. Then, as she gazed at the creature's face, she suddenly felt her head swim. When she looked up again, Cameron and James were staring at her with worried looks.

'Are you OK?' James asked, his face full of concern.

Mandy nodded. 'It's just that . . . well, the markings on its face remind me of a wolf that I've seen before,' she said cautiously. She was unsure of what Cameron might think, if she told him about her wolf.

James immediately understood. 'It's a mark like a T, isn't it?'

'There's a story behind this wolf,' Cameron began enthusiastically. 'One winter, Fiona was staying here, getting over an illness. Because she hadn't been out for so long, some of the wild animals came close to the house, to see what was wrong. Fiona saw them and went out to join them. But,' he paused to looked at their rapt faces, 'she wandered much further than she should've done and became weak.'

Mandy looked at the drawing more closely. The girl certainly looked frail and delicate. 'Go on,' she urged Cameron. 'What happened?'

'Well, when it was realised that she was missing, a search party was formed and they went out to find her. In those days, people were frightened of wild animals and the hunters in the party carried guns . . .' He paused again and looked from Mandy to James.

Mandy frowned. She had a horrible feeling that she wasn't going to like the next part of this story.

'Eventually, they spotted her. She was fast asleep, leaning against a log. But when they got nearer, they saw that it wasn't a log. A huge old wolf was lying right beside her, almost covering her. It sprang up when it saw them coming and started to walk away from them.' Cameron stopped speaking.

'And?' Mandy pleaded softly.

'Because wolves were considered a menace, the hunters shot it dead,' Cameron said, his voice cracking slightly. 'But, when they reached Fiona, she was warm and dry, even though it was snowing heavily. They realised then that the old wolf had been protecting her. It had been keeping her warm with its body and tail. Some of the men felt very guilty about what had happened.'

'So they should!' Mandy said fiercely. 'What a *terrible* thing to do. It sounds as if the wolf knew that Fiona would be safe and was leaving to let the search party look after her.'

'Were there any other wolves around?' James asked very quietly.

'That's another thing, James,' Cameron said with a grimace. 'Wolves were never seen again on the Mudie Estate after that. There was talk that Fiona's wolf could even have been the last wolf in Scotland.'

'What happened to Fiona?' Mandy asked.

'She was distraught,' Cameron said. 'She was in such a state that they thought she would become ill again. That's when they gave her the sketchbook, where she drew a beautiful portrait of the wolf. But, it's said that she was so upset about the wolf's death, her tears dropped on the page and the ink ran. To try and cheer her up, they had the doorknocker copied from her sketch. Did you notice it on the front door?'

'We certainly did!' Mandy said. 'It gave me a shock.'

'Why?' Cameron said, looking surprised.

'Erm . . . well . . .' Mandy stuttered, swallowing hard. 'I just wasn't expecting it, that's all.'

'Oh, I see,' Cameron said politely, giving her a strange look. 'Let me show you the portrait of the wolf, then.' He turned to the next page. 'That's funny,' he exclaimed, looking baffled. 'It should be the next picture.' Frowning, Cameron turned the pages back and forth. 'There's just a blank page here.'

'What are those marks?' Mandy stared hard at the blank page. 'Look, there are grey splodges on the page.'

'I don't know,' Cameron admitted. 'I've never noticed this page before. It's much thinner than the other pages, too.'

'It's almost transparent, like glass,' Mandy observed.

'That's very odd . . .' Cameron frowned, looking through the pictures a second time. 'I'll put it away and ask my parents about it later. Maybe they've taken the page out for some reason.' He wrapped the book in the black tissue. 'This stops the light getting to it and fading the pictures,' he said, climbing back on to the stool and replacing the box.

An hour later, they were in Cameron's bedroom looking at his school project, when they heard a *toot-toot-toot* from outside.

'I promised I'd give Mum a hand with the bags,' Cameron said, quickly getting up.

'We'll help too,' Mandy offered. They followed him out of the back door where Cameron's mum was unloading suitcases and holdalls from the car.

'You must be Mandy and James?' Mrs Mudie said, brushing her dark brown hair back with a gloved hand. 'We're so pleased you could all come. It's going to be a lovely party. Dad's taken our guests up to see the deer,' she told Cameron, as they picked up the cases.

When all the bags had been taken up to the Minstrels' Gallery, Mandy and James decided that it was time for them to go. Cameron saw them to the door.

'Cameron, tell me one more thing,' Mandy asked him. 'What happened to Fiona?'

'He took a very deep breath. 'She married my great, great, great, great, great, great, great,

great-grandfather,' he said, 'so her blood is in the Mudie clan.'

'How many greats was that?' James said with a gulp.

'Eight,' Cameron said, laughing. 'But so far, no one in the family has inherited her way with wild animals!'

'Your dad's a vet, though,' Mandy pointed out.

'It's not quite the same thing,' Cameron said. 'Dad says that Fiona's gift was very rare and special. See you tonight,' he said, then gave a wicked grin. 'You might not recognise me!'

Seven

'I can't believe that Fiona's wolf and our wolf look *so* alike!' Mandy burst out, as soon as the door had closed behind them.

'*And* the doorknocker!' James exclaimed, stopping in his tracks. 'Its eyes seem to follow you wherever you go.'

Mandy turned to look at him. 'I know,' she said, sighing deeply. 'There's something very spooky going on, but I haven't a clue what it is.'

'Do you think there *is* a connection between the wolves?' James said uneasily. He ran his hand through his hair and stared hard at Mandy. 'But how *can* there be a connection?' he asked, shaking his head. 'The wolf in the picture is dead, isn't it? And ours is alive – we've seen it!'

'I just don't know,' Mandy answered. 'All the time we were looking at Cameron's project, I couldn't stop wondering about all the strange things that keep happening,' she added, absent-mindedly tapping the heel of her boot on a frozen puddle. 'I know that our wolf wants something. I can see it in its eyes.'

'Maybe we ought to tell your mum and dad?' James suggested.

'I thought about that, but they'd just worry,' Mandy reasoned, setting off down the track again.

'Suppose we *never* find out what it's all about?' James exclaimed suddenly.

'It's happening for a reason,' Mandy said confidently. 'I'm sure of that.'

When they arrived at the lodge, the winter sun had almost disappeared and Mr Hope was setting the table.

'We're having a really late lunch because there will be lots of food at the party,' he said cheerfully. 'I've made a big omelette, Spanish style with tatties. It'll be delicious.'

'You're muddling up your countries, Dad,' Mandy laughed.

After lunch Mandy and James washed up while Mrs Hope went to unpack their clothes for the big night.

'James, you'd better take Blackie out for some air. He's improving in leaps and bounds,' Mr Hope said. 'But he's going to be shut in again this evening.'

'Hi, Mum,' Mandy said, going into the bedroom and flopping on the bed.

'There, that's the last thing to be ironed,' Emily Hope said to her daughter, as she put James's shirt on a coat hanger. 'Would you mind taking it upstairs for me please? And here's your new trousers and top. We'll have to start getting ready soon – I can't wait!'

'I'm looking forward to it too,' laughed Mandy. But in the back of her mind, she couldn't stop thinking about the wolf she had seen. She took the hangers from her mum and carried them carefully upstairs, hanging James's shirt on the back of his door.

Then she went into her room. *Brrrrrr!* She couldn't believe how icy it was. Quickly hanging up her clothes, Mandy stooped to feel the radiator. It was hot! But she was so cold that she was shivering.

Mandy shook herself. She was letting the wolf get to her so much that she was starting to imagine things. Obviously, she hadn't shut the window properly. She was just crossing the room to check it, when the lights began to flicker. Quickly, she looked around for the candle, but at once the room was plunged into inky blackness. Moonlight flickered through the window. The eerie silver light seemed to dance on the walls and the carpet.

Mandy knew that she should go downstairs and get a torch, but she couldn't move. She heard James come stomping up the stairs to his room. She desperately wanted to call out to him, but she couldn't speak. She felt as if icy cold fingers were creeping down her spine.

What is happening to me? Mandy thought desperately. And then, from just outside the window came a noise. *Clang!* She felt her heart leap with fear. It was a trap clamping shut!

Turning her head, she stared out of the window – and could hardly believe her eyes.

On the other side of the track, not twenty metres from the lodge and as clear as day in the sharp moonlight, was a wolf. Stealthily and cautiously, it walked out from among the trees and loped down towards the loch. It was followed by another. Then more and more wolves appeared, until a whole wolf pack was streaming out of the forest. The powerful muscles beneath their glossy coats rippled in the moonlight. At the loch, they stopped to drink.

Mandy stood mesmerised.

Then, out of the corner of her eye, she spotted movement in the forest. Her heart skipped a beat, then thudded hard. Suppose it was the poachers who'd seen the wolves? What if they were setting *more* traps? Then, out of the dark wood padded a splendid creature, bigger than any other in the pack.

'*The old wolf!*' Mandy gasped. The animal met her gaze and, as she watched, the others gathered behind it. So, the old wolf with the yellow eyes was the alpha wolf, the head of the pack.

Suddenly, the lights in the room came back on, and in a flash the eerie scene vanished. Mandy pressed her nose against the window to peer out, but the landscape was bleak and empty. Not a wolf was in sight.

'James!' At once, Mandy ran out and tapped urgently on his door. She was filled with a strange combination of both fear and excitement.

'What's happened?' James said, as he opened the door and saw her face shining with excitement.

'Quick, come with me,' Mandy hissed. She ran downstairs, opened the front door quietly and ran swiftly towards the loch.

'Hey, go steady,' James said as he caught up

with her. 'What's it all about?'

'When I went into my room just now, it was freezing cold,' Mandy hurriedly explained. 'Then, when the lights went out, I saw the old wolf.' Catching her breath, her voice trailed off as she saw the look on James's face. 'He had a wolf pack with him – and they stood here . . .' she finished lamely.

'But they didn't go off,' James said, puzzled. 'The lights I mean, they were on all the time.' He frowned and looked down at the ground. 'And there are no footprints, or anything,' he said quietly.

'Well, the lights went off in *my* room, and I saw the wolves!' Mandy said, in a furious voice. '*What* is going on?'

'Maybe we *should* tell your parents,' James said quietly.

Mandy nodded, pushing her hands deep into her pockets. 'I would, normally,' she said. 'But what's to tell? They think that I imagined the wolf. How can I tell them that I've now seen a whole pack?'

'That's true,' James agreed. 'We don't have anything concrete, do we?'

When they got back, Adam and Emily Hope

were getting ready for the party, so Mandy and James went upstairs to get changed too. Putting on her new turquoise trousers and top, Mandy decided to put all thought of wolves out of her mind until the next morning.

'Aren't we a smart bunch?' Adam Hope said, with a lopsided grin. Both he and James wore crisp white shirts and dark trousers. Emily Hope looked very smart in a vivid green silk dress.

'Bye, Blackie,' Mandy said, scratching the Labrador behind his ears, as James came in from the kitchen.

'A special treat,' James told him, laying a plate of dog biscuits beside Blackie's bed.

They collected their coats, locked the door and set off for the main house.

As they turned into the drive, they could hear the faint sound of music. Mandy looked at James and grinned. She felt better already. Two people were greeting guests at the door, but Mandy didn't know either of them. They both wore tweed jackets, tartan kilts, white knee-high socks and black leather shoes that laced around their ankles. It wasn't until they drew closer that Mandy suddenly realised the doormen were Angus and Cameron.

'You were right,' she said, her eyes shining with amusement. 'I *didn't* recognise you at all. You look *so* different in a kilt.'

'At least you didn't call it a skirt!' Cameron said. 'Some people do. This is the Mudie tartan,' he told them proudly.

'Welcome, welcome!' Angus Mudie boomed. He invited them inside and closed the door. 'You're about the last, I think.'

Angus put his arms round Adam and Emily's shoulders and led them into the Great Hall. The tables were groaning with plates and bowls of delicious food. Meanwhile, up in the gallery, a band was providing background music.

'Help yourselves to whatever you want,' Angus said to Mandy and James. 'I'll take your parents off for a drink, first.'

They joined the queue of people and had soon piled their plates high. Then they found somewhere to sit and eat.

'Look,' Mandy said, nudging James. 'See that man in the green kilt by the stairs?' She waited till James saw him.

'It's that man who was in the shop complaining about the wolves,' James said softly, finishing the last chunk of garlic bread on his plate.

Mandy nodded. 'Brett McCatter. And there's Donald from the mini-market,' she said, nodding towards the window. He was standing with a woman wearing a long skirt in a tartan that matched his kilt. Donald saw Mandy looking over and waved. She waved back at once, smiling.

When everybody had finished eating, waiters collected the plates and cleared the tables. Then there was a drum roll from up in the balcony and one of the musicians stood up.

'Pray silence for the piper,' he announced, in a booming voice.

Within seconds, everyone was waiting expectantly. The door behind them opened and the ghostly wail of bagpipes playing 'Happy Birthday' rang out. Then a piper in full regalia appeared, followed by two men carrying an enormous birthday cake decorated with blazing candles. They all joined in singing and Mandy could hear her dad's strong voice above all the others. Angus blew out the candles and everybody cheered. As Mrs Mudie began cutting the cake into slices, Cameron came over.

'Could you two help me hand the cake round?' he asked.

'I can hardly move,' Mandy joked. 'I've eaten too much.'

'Me too,' James added.

'Then the exercise will do you good!' Cameron laughed. 'Come on.'

At the table, they collected trays covered with pieces of cake wrapped in serviettes and offered them to all of the guests. They had just finished when the musician announced that there would be dancing in a few moments. Everyone immediately formed themselves into groups and waited for the music to start.

'Come on, James,' Emily Hope said, grabbing his arm. 'You can be my partner.'

James blushed, but followed Mrs Hope. Adam Hope offered Mandy his arm and they too found a space on the crowded dance floor. Soon they were laughing fit to burst, as they tried to copy the steps and follow the rest of the dancers. It seemed as if they'd only just begun, when the last dance of the night was announced.

'But I was just getting the hang of it!' protested Adam Hope, gasping with laughter.

'I don't think I've got the energy for this,' Emily Hope admitted. 'It's been wonderful, but

I'm exhausted.'

'You have to dance the last one,' Adam Hope said linking his arm in hers. 'I'll hold you up. It's bound to be a slow one!'

But the music got faster and faster and soon everybody was dancing wildly, spinning about the hall. Mandy lost sight of her mum and dad and just managed to hang on to James's arm. When the dance ended, they all clapped and cheered. The band continued to play popular Scottish tunes, as Mandy sank in a chair to get her breath back. Lots of people still seemed to have some energy left and stood about the room, chatting to each other.

'Phew, I'm tired,' Cameron said as he joined them. 'Did you enjoy the dancing?' He looked hot and flung his jacket on a chair as he sat down.

'Great fun,' Mandy answered. 'But pretty energetic.' She almost had to shout to be heard over the noisy hubbub in the room. 'Why didn't Sally and Duncan come?'

'They had to go to Edinburgh today for an important conference on wildlife parks,' Cameron said. 'It's been arranged for a long time. They said that they'll call in on their way home if they have time.' He frowned suddenly.

'What's the matter?' Mandy asked.

Cameron stood up. 'I thought I heard someone knocking,' he said, crossing to the door.

Mandy and James heard it too. *Bang, bang, bang.*

Cameron peered around the door. 'What's up, Gary?' he asked, opening the door to reveal a young man wearing dirty blue overalls and muddy boots. His red hair was lank and greasy and he had a furious expression on his face. Pushing past Cameron, he strode in to the Great Hall. Everyone fell silent as he appeared.

'There's trouble in the wildlife park!' he shouted, so that everyone could hear. 'The wolves have got out,' he explained, looking at the astonished faces around him.

'I'm sure it's nothing to worry about,' said Donald's wife. 'Duncan and Sally will soon have them back in the enclosure.'

Several people in the crowd nodded agreement and began to move around again, murmuring to each other, but Gary had more to say.

'No! You don't understand!' he yelled, and every head turned to him again. 'The wolves have escaped from the *wildlife park* – they're running wild in the woods. None of the livestock is safe.'

A hush fell on the room broken only by one man's voice.

'I knew it!' he thundered. The crowd parted and a man came striding towards the door. He thumped his fist on the nearest table, making glasses and bottles rattle together. 'I *said* this would happen – and I've been proved right!'

In a flash Mandy was on her feet with James, craning to see the angry man. Her spirits sank when she saw that it was Brett McCatter.

'They've got to be stopped, and stopped for good!' he went on ominously, looking around the room. 'We can't chance this happening again. Who's coming with me?'

'I am,' a voice came from the back. Mandy recognised the man from the shop who owned a herd of deer.

'And us!' Two men standing nearby stepped forward.

'Me too,' Gary added.

'Let's go then,' McCatter said. 'I've got my guns in the van.'

Mandy looked desperately around for her parents. Normally, her dad would try to defuse such a situation. But the Hopes were nowhere in sight.

'My dad will have something to say about this,' Cameron said boldly, standing in front of McCatter. 'After all, it's his wildlife park.'

'But the wolves are not *in* the park any more,' McCatter spat out, waving him aside. 'That's the trouble.'

Everybody surged forward.

'We've got to stop them,' Mandy said urgently to James and Cameron, who were staring in horror at the group of men hurrying out of the door. They all knew what would happen to the young wolves when they were found. 'James, can you look for Cameron's parents and Mum and Dad? Tell them what's happening. We'll try and stall Brett and his gang!'

'Right,' James said, with a firm nod. He headed back into the crush.

Mandy and Cameron pushed their way through the crowd and burst out of the front door. The men were climbing into the big green van.

'Stop,' Mandy cried out, grabbing Brett McCatter's sleeve. 'You can't shoot the wolves. They're only young. They haven't done any harm.'

'Get off me!' McCatter growled, wrenching his sleeve from Mandy's grasp and sending her sprawling back against Cameron. 'What do you know about it anyway? I'll not have a lass telling *me* what to do,' he sneered.

'Huh,' she snorted, running to the back of the van and peering in. She could see at least three guns fixed to the side of the van. 'He must have planned this, Cameron,' she said, her voice stiff with anger. 'We've got to stop him.'

'How can we?' Cameron asked, as the door slammed shut. 'They're going now.'

James came rushing up to them as the van roared into life and began to move off.

'I can't find *any* of your parents,' he gasped, out of breath. 'I looked everywhere. Someone said that Mr Mudie was showing your mum and dad around. They could be anywhere.'

'OK. We'll have to do it without them,' decided Mandy. She turned to Cameron. 'Is there any way we can get to the park before McCatter?'

'Yes, through the woods – do you remember where Blackie was hurt?' Cameron said. Then he frowned. 'Why?'

'Because *we've* got to get there first,' she said, starting forward. 'We've *got* to find the wolves. Come on!'

Eight

'Hang on, Mandy!' James protested. 'We can't go running about in the woods if there's an armed gang lurking!'

'But we *have* to go,' Mandy said impatiently. 'If we get there first, they won't go around shooting things.'

'I'd like to believe that,' Cameron said. 'But Brett McCatter can be a nasty piece of work. He wasn't even invited tonight. He just sort of gatecrashed and Dad felt it would be bad manners to turn him away.'

'Mandy, we can't go without telling your parents. We promised not to go into the woods,' James said.

'Right, I'll look for them,' she agreed. 'James, if you fetch our coats, I'll find Mum and Dad. Meet you back here.'

'You've only got a couple of minutes, Mandy,' Cameron warned her. 'After that, it will be too late to beat the van to the wildlife park.'

Mandy sped up the steps and scanned the Great Hall. Her parents were nowhere to be seen. Time was running out for the wolves. She made a snap decision and, picking up a white paper napkin, she ran over to Donald.

'Have you got a pen?' she asked quickly.

The shopkeeper reached in his inside pocket and pulled out a Biro. 'Can we help at all?' he said kindly. 'Are you worried about the wolves?'

Mandy nodded. 'Yes,' she said, scribbling a note on the napkin.

Gone to the park to look for the wolves. Couldn't find you. Don't worry – we'll be careful. Love Mandy.

She handed back the pen, and folded the paper napkin. 'Could you give this to my parents, please?' she asked Donald and his wife. Their name is Hope – I think they're with Angus.' Thrusting the note into his hand, she dashed out of the front door.

'Let's go!' Mandy shouted to James and Cameron as she flew down the steps. James passed her coat to her and she shrugged it on quickly.

'What did your parents say?' James quizzed her as they ran. 'I thought they'd come with us. Are they driving to the wildlife park?'

'I couldn't find them, actually,' Mandy said breathlessly. Cameron was running really quickly.

'What?' James exclaimed, skidding to a halt. 'I don't believe it!'

'I did leave them a note,' Mandy called back. 'They'll understand that we don't have any choice. We *can't* let the wolves die! Now let's get a move on!' she said, forging ahead.

When James caught up with her, she was standing above a brook, while Cameron clambered down the bank below them.

'This is a short cut to the park, but be careful,' he called up. 'It's very slippery because the mud has frozen over.'

Mandy inched her way down the steep bank, clutching at plants and bushes to stop herself from sliding out of control. At the bottom, she and Cameron waited for James, before they all waded across the stream.

'Aah,' Mandy gave an involuntary gasp. 'It's freezing.' Her new trousers were wet up to her knees. Her best shoes were soaking now and covered with mud.

They climbed up the bank on the other side. Mandy's fingers were so cold that they hurt. Her shoes were rubbing blisters. But none of the discomfort mattered. The important thing was to get to the wolves before the hunting party.

The track they were following had narrowed until they had to run in single file. Mandy felt her trousers catch on a bramble and rip. Cameron's socks were round his ankles and James's dark trousers were covered with mud.

Suddenly, there was a loud shriek as a startled bird flew into the air. Instantly, Mandy remembered the sound of the trap clanging shut.

'Cameron, slow down,' she panted as he tore along in front of her. 'Don't forget that there could be traps set round here.'

'We're nearly at the perimeter fence between the estate and the wildlife park,' Cameron said softly, slowing to a walk and pointing ahead of them. 'Look, there it is.'

'But it looks funny,' James said, pushing his glasses firmly on to his nose. 'It's not standing up straight.'

'It's a gap – there's a big gap!' Mandy said horrified as they reached it. 'In both fences. No wonder the wolves got out.'

'The fences have been cut!' James said. 'Look at the edges.'

'They've used bolt cutters,' Cameron observed bitterly. 'They'll go through *anything*.'

'Let's start searching the woods,' Mandy said, her mouth set in a grim line. 'It's more important than ever that we find the young wolves. McCatter obviously means to shoot them whatever happens.'

'Mandy, look!' Cameron clutched her arm as she started to move off. She turned swiftly and looked in the direction he was pointing. Lights were moving towards them. And they were getting closer.

'Headlights!' she muttered darkly. Mandy felt a shiver of fear. McCatter's gang was getting very close. 'Come on!' she shouted. 'We've got to find them first!'

Spreading out, but still keeping each other in view, they began walking slowly into the darkest parts of the wood. Mandy looked back over her shoulder. The lights had stopped moving. As she watched, they went out completely. The hunters had arrived.

Nine

Mandy started forwards again. James was on her left and Cameron to her right. In the wintry night, hardly anything moved. An owl flew above their heads and peered down inquisitively at them. Suddenly Mandy stopped and waited. The other two drew nearer to her.

'Look ahead,' she whispered. 'I'm sure I saw a movement – it was up there by the oak tree.' They crept on as silently as they could. Mandy felt nervous, but she *had* to keep calm. She mustn't frighten off the wolves!

'Whaaaaarrr!' Something gave a loud angry wail right in front of them. Mandy clutched her throat with shock and stood rigid.

Suddenly, a snarling creature with a blunt-ended tail shot up a tree. It stopped on a branch with its hackles raised, flashing its eyes at Mandy. It looked so furious that, for one awful moment, Mandy thought it was going to launch itself straight at her head.

'It's a wildcat,' Cameron whispered. 'They're very, very dangerous. Even the kittens are fierce.'

Under normal circumstances, nothing could have dragged Mandy from the wildcat, but tonight she had a more important task. Continuing through the forest, they disturbed several rabbits and one disgruntled hare. Mandy glanced over her shoulder every few seconds. Occasionally she saw the flicker of a light, but nothing more. She waited for the boom of a gunshot, but didn't hear a sound.

Leading the way, Mandy struggled through a huge bramble patch. She felt the thorns scratching at her legs and tugging at her clothes. Bitter tears of frustration welled up in her eyes. How could they have been so stupid? They had *no* chance of finding the wolves in such large woods.

At long last, she freed herself from the brambles. Wiping her face with a sleeve, she peered into the darkness. And two pairs of yellow eyes stared back at her.

It was the wolves!

Holding their tails in the air, the young wolves growled and bared their fangs. The three searchers stood very still. The wolves wouldn't let Mandy get any closer. She could hardly believe these were the same animals that she had stroked and played with yesterday.

'We're here to help you,' Mandy said softly at last. 'You have to let us.' Almost as if they were reassured by her voice, the wolves trotted a few paces away, then turned to watch her, ears pricked. But as Mandy moved towards them they ran off again.

'Oh no,' she groaned to James and Cameron. 'Now they want to play games. We'll have to follow them – we can't lose them now!'

Sprinting after the wolves and trying desperately to keep them in sight, Mandy lost all sense of direction. But, at last, they slowed down.

'Where are we?' Mandy asked Cameron, as he and James caught up.

'We're still on estate land, but we've moved away from the park,' Cameron answered. 'That's good for the wolves. I doubt that McCatter will stray too far from the wildlife park.' But, as he said it, James pointed at the wolves.

'Look,' he urged. 'I think they've spotted something.'

The young wolves had stopped to sniff the ground. Mandy, James and Cameron stood stock-still, watching. Then, to their horror, the wolves turned back towards the park. There was nothing they could do except follow them. Mandy felt her heart sink as the wolves began loping through the woods, so quickly and silently that they could only just keep them in sight. They were heading straight into danger!

'They're slowing,' James panted. 'Look, there's something moving up ahead.'

Mandy stopped quickly and crept closer to the wolves. Now she could see the shape of a rabbit up ahead. 'They're hunting,' she said. 'They can't miss from that distance. But the wolves were young and this was their first hunt. They were so excited that they began wagging their tails. Immediately, the rabbit saw them. In a flash it sprang up and bolted into a burrow.

The wolves stood pawing at the ground.

'Aren't they funny!' Mandy could hardly hold in her laughter.

'Let's see if we can get closer to them,' said James.

At the burrow, the wolves were still busily trying to make the rabbit come out. The black wolf barked with frustration.

Mandy gasped. 'Don't,' she called to them. 'Don't let the hunters know where you are.'

The wolves stared across at Mandy. To her dismay, they pricked up their ears and trotted away once more. 'Not again!' she said, and went after them. Then she stopped so abruptly that James almost crashed into her.

Mandy felt every sense in her body go to red alert. Ahead of the wolves, half-buried in the ground, was the glint of metal – a trap.

But, to her immense relief, the wolves stopped before they reached the trap. Then they turned and watched the three followers.

'What's wrong?' James asked softly.

'There,' Mandy nodded toward the wolves. 'Look behind them, at the bottom of the tree.'

'It's a trap!' Cameron declared, his voice grim. 'You can just see the plate in the middle.'

'We have to draw them away from it,' Mandy said. 'Maybe if we back off, they might follow.'

'It's worth a try,' said James.

Carefully they stepped backwards until there was more space between them and the wolves.

'Please,' Mandy begged under her breath. 'Please come to us. Don't go the other way. It's *so* dangerous.'

'Come on!' she heard Cameron mutter. 'Come here.'

But the wolves seemed to have lost interest in them. Now that Mandy wouldn't play games, they began to wander off. 'What else can we do?' she muttered to herself. She thought for a moment. 'What if we approached them from the opposite direction?' she whispered to the others. 'Then they might move *away* from the wildlife park. We've been chasing them towards it!'

'I'll go,' James offered.

Then, before James could move, Cameron laid a hand on his arm. 'I think it's too late. Look!'

The wobbling light of torches was coming straight for them.

'Could it be Mum and Dad?' Mandy suggested.

Cameron shook his head. 'I don't think so. They'd call out, wouldn't they?'

Mandy nodded. 'It's McCatter,' she said in a miserable voice. She felt desperate. And then she felt a strange sensation pricking at the back of her neck. The young wolves began jumping around and acting skittishly. Then they stopped very still – it was as if their fur was standing on end.

'They must have heard the hunters,' Cameron said quietly.

Mandy suddenly sensed something close by – she could tell that the wolves felt it too. A cloud blocked out the moon, casting the forest in darkness. In vain, they craned forward to see the wolves, but the cloud passed and moonlight shone down again.

Between the trap and the wolves stood a huge animal.

'Where did *that* come from?' said Cameron in amazement.

Mandy didn't answer. Her eyes were locked on to those of the old wolf. He met her gaze for a few seconds and then looked away towards the young wolves, baring his teeth. Instantly, they flattened their ears and tucked their tails between their legs. They began to creep towards him, keeping their bodies low to the ground. But the old wolf bared his fangs at them again and the young wolves veered off towards Mandy.

She stepped forward. The young wolves turned and looked back at the old wolf, then went up to Mandy and stood waiting. Tears stung her eyes as she looked at the old wolf. 'I'll keep them safe,' she whispered to him.

'Mandy,' she heard James call softly. 'Hurry up – the gang's coming.'

She grabbed the young grey wolf by its thick scruff, gesturing to James to hold the other, and they all crouched down as low as they could behind some prickly bushes. The old grey wolf was standing his ground, apparently quite unconcerned that the hunters were approaching.

Go away! Mandy willed the old wolf to go, but still he stood there.

The torchlight was very close now and they could make out figures coming through the woods.

'They're here,' Mandy said, clutching the young wolf's scruff.

'Will you look at that?' they heard Brett

McCatter laugh. 'It's just waiting for us.'

'But that's not a young wolf,' one of the other hunters said.

'That wolf is much older,' they heard another man say in a nervous voice. 'And a big one at that. Where has it come from, McCatter?'

'Who cares?' McCatter cut in. 'It's a wolf – and the only safe wolf is a dead one.'

'*Booooom!*' A single shot rang out, deafeningly loud in the still night air.

The old wolf stood watching the hunters, not moving a muscle.

'How could I have missed it?' Brett McCatter's voice was now tense and panicky. 'Fire!' he shouted. 'Everyone, fire!'

Shots rang out from the guns and echoed throughout the woods.

When the firing had stopped, Mandy could hardly bear to look.

'Why doesn't it fall?' said a frantic voice. 'We've peppered it with enough lead to kill *twenty* wolves.'

To Mandy's amazement, the old wolf was still standing there, motionless. He'd raised his hackles, making him look even bigger, and his yellow eyes seemed to glow in the darkness.

Somehow, he didn't look old any more.

'We couldn't have missed him, not at that range,' another of the men said, his voice trembling with fear.

'I'm going! I don't want to be involved with this,' shouted someone else, throwing down his gun.

Mandy could see that their faces were chalk-white in the moonlight as they ran away, leaving McCatter alone. He stared at the wolf as if he were hypnotised. The old wolf raised his head, looked up at the sky and started to howl. At once, the air was filled with the deafening sound of hundreds of wolves howling! Mandy shivered uncontrollably.

Then, abruptly, the sound stopped. Brett McCatter backed away with a look of sheer terror as the old wolf began to walk slowly towards him – its eyes blazing.

McCatter stood rigid, unable to look away, unable to turn and run after his companions. His knees trembled and the gun fell from his grasp on to the ground. The old wolf was now only five metres away from him, advancing ever closer.

Mandy stood watching, holding tight to the young wolf.

'Will it attack?' James asked her.

'I don't know,' murmured Mandy.

With a cry, McCatter broke free from the huge animal's hypnotic gaze. Then, he turned and ran for his life. He crashed recklessly through the undergrowth, stumbling headlong into a ditch, to emerge seconds later covered in mud. Then he was up and running again.

The old wolf watched calmly, as McCatter disappeared among the trees. Then he turned to face Mandy. She met the old wolf's eyes, somehow knowing that this would be the last time that she'd see him. He shifted his gaze to the young wolves.

Mandy knelt down and put an arm round each animal. 'Trust me,' she said, looking up.

But the old wolf had melted away among the trees.

Ten

They were silent as they walked back to Cameron's house. The young wolves also seemed subdued. It had been a strange time for them all. They were almost home when they saw the lights of torches coming towards them. For a second, Mandy worried that it might be the gang, but reason told her that they would be much too scared to come back.

'Mandy! James!' Adam Hope's voice thundered out.

'Cameron, is that you?' It was Angus Mudie.

'Over here, Dad!' Mandy called, exchanging

nervous glances with James and Cameron. 'We've got the wolves with us – they're safe.'

'Mandy Hope, you've gone too far this time!' Adam Hope said in an angry voice as he hurried over. 'Your note gave us a terrible shock. Then we heard gunshots! We daren't imagine *what* might be happening!'

'We didn't have any choice. There wasn't enough time, Dad,' Mandy explained, her voice flustered. 'The gang had already left and I *did* look for you, honestly.'

'We only just got there in the nick of time, Mr Hope,' Cameron said. 'McCatter was out to kill the wolves.'

'That's all very well, Cameron,' Mr Hope said. 'But there were guns involved!' He put his hands on his hips and stared at them. 'And what about your promise, Mandy?'

Mandy looked up at her dad's face. 'I'm really sorry, Dad,' she said, looking down at the ground, realising what great risks they'd taken. 'I didn't mean to worry you, but the wolves were in such danger . . .'

'. . . that you had to act first and think later,' said Adam Hope, finishing the sentence for her. 'But you're all safe and sound, so I suppose that's all that really matters,' he said, relenting and giving Mandy a hug.

'I must admit that without you, these young wolves would almost certainly be dead,' Angus Mudie said with a grudging smile. 'PC Farish has gone after McCatter and his gang,' he told them. 'He's promised to let us know as soon as he catches up with them.

'What shall we do about the wolves?' Cameron asked his father.

'Duncan and Sally are on their way,' Angus told them. 'They were too late back to come to the party, so they went straight home. They were horrified to find that the wolves had gone. They telephoned and I told them we were just going out to search for you.'

Duncan and Sally were in the drive, talking anxiously to Pat Mudie and Emily Hope, when they arrived back. Immediately, Mandy's mum and Mrs Mudie came flying down the steps towards the bedraggled group.

'Mandy, you gave us such a scare! I was worried frantic when I heard the shots.' Emily Hope said, hugging her daughter tightly.

Mrs Mudie sighed and put an arm round

Cameron. 'Whatever were you thinking of, dashing off like that?'

'They were going to shoot the wolves, Mum,' Cameron said. 'We had to stop them.'

'And you did, didn't you?' Mrs Mudie said, with a trace of pride in her voice. 'But look at the state of you all!' she said. 'You must be frozen. I'll go and make everyone a nice hot drink.'

'Not for us, Pat,' Sally called after her. She was putting leads on the wolves. 'I can't imagine how they got out, Mandy, but you did wonderfully well to find them *and* to make them come with you. How on earth did you manage it?'

'We had a bit of help from—' Mandy stopped mid-sentence. Then, seeing Sally's puzzled look, she hurriedly added, 'Someone had cut a big hole in the fence – *that's* how they got out.'

'Someone *wanted* them to get out,' James said, darkly.

'Cut a hole in the fence?' Duncan repeated, stomping angrily round the van. 'That's a criminal offence – I'll make sure that the police know about this!' Then he looked towards the two wolves and sighed. 'We'd better get these two home now,' he said, laying a blanket in the back of the van.

Mandy helped Sally lead the wolves over to the van. They looked up at her as she stroked them both, then held their heads close. 'I don't know who he was, but he saved your lives *twice* tonight,' she whispered to them, suddenly realising that it had gone very quiet behind her. As she turned round, she saw that everyone was staring at her.

'You have a rare way with animals, Mandy,' Angus Mudie said thoughtfully. 'A rare way indeed.'

'You certainly get along with these two,' agreed Duncan, coaxing the wolves into the van and closing the doors. 'Thank you *all* for your help tonight,' he added.

As they trooped inside, James nudged Mandy. 'What are you going to say about the old wolf?'

'I don't know yet,' she replied.

'Here we are,' Pat Mudie announced, coming out of the kitchen. 'Hot fruit punch to warm you up.'

'Will you take a wee dram of whisky in yours, Adam?' Angus Mudie asked.

Adam Hope nodded. 'Just a small one,

Angus,' he said smiling. 'After all, I've had quite a shock tonight. By the way, James . . .' He paused as James looked over at him. 'It did cross my mind how I might explain all this to your parents, should anything have happened to you out there.'

James blushed pink.

'As it is, we'll have to explain how you managed to ruin your best trousers!' said Mr Hope, trying to smother a grin.

But before anyone could say anything, there was a tap on the door. It was PC Farish. Mrs Mudie gave him a hot drink and they all sat around waiting expectantly for his news.

'Thank you, Pat,' PC Farish said, taking a sip of the punch. 'Now, I certainly don't wish to encourage such reckless behaviour, but I have to admit that between you,' he looked from Mandy and James to Cameron, 'you did a pretty good night's work.'

Mandy grinned. 'Did you catch McCatter and the others?'

'Thanks to you, I certainly did!' PC Farish explained. 'It turns out that McCatter planned this as soon as the wolves arrived. The party gave him the opportunity he needed. Half the neighbourhood was here and everyone knew that Duncan and Sally would be away. The coast was clear. McCatter cut the fences, then came on to the party leaving Gary Kemp to raise the alarm. Incidentally, he works for him on the farm.'

'So McCatter had it all planned out,' sighed Mr Hope. 'Right down to the last detail.'

'Almost. But he couldn't have known that these youngsters would get the wolves to safety before he was even on the scene,' PC Farish said with a chuckle.

'They were shooting at . . .' Cameron burst out, but was quickly silenced by a look from Mandy. 'Aren't you going to arrest them?' he continued.

'They're all down at the station now, waiting to be charged,' PC Farish said. 'When I found him, McCatter was on his knees, shaking from head to toe. He was babbling incoherently about haunted woods, ghostly wolves and all sorts of strange things. He says that he'll never set foot in the woods again, not as long as he lives!'

'Haunted woods?' Angus Mudie declared. 'Ghosts? Nonsense! I've walked in those woods for years and I've never seen anything out of the ordinary. The man's gone mad.'

Mandy, James and Cameron looked at each other knowingly.

PC Farish spotted the exchange of glances. 'Did any of you see anything suspicious or dangerous in the woods this evening?' he asked, looking Mandy straight in the eye.

'No,' Mandy replied honestly. As far as she was concerned, there was nothing suspicious or dangerous about the old wolf. 'The only dangerous thing was McCatter.'

'Well, then,' PC Farish said, standing up and putting on his cap. 'I'll go and see Duncan in the morning. He'll have charges of his own to add, no doubt. McCatter won't forget *this* party in a hurry!'

Mandy turned to Cameron when the policeman had left the room. 'Did you find the picture of the wolf that you were telling us about?' she asked.

'I haven't told Mum that it's missing yet,' Cameron replied.

'What's missing?' Mrs Mudie asked.

'The portrait of Fiona's wolf,' Cameron said. 'I showed Mandy and James the sketchbook and it wasn't there.'

'Of course it's there, Cameron,' Mrs Mudie smiled. 'Where else would it be? It's been there for hundreds of years – it's hardly likely to go missing on its own now, is it?'

'Honestly Mum, it *wasn't* there,' said Cameron, looking at Mandy and James for confirmation. 'Was it?'

'It wasn't, Mrs Mudie,' Mandy agreed. 'There was just an empty page.'

'An empty page?' Mrs Mudie looked puzzled. 'Angus, could you get the book down, please? Let's sort this out.'

'What is this sketchbook?' Mrs Hope asked.

'Fiona was a young girl who was sent here to recover from the ague in the eighteenth century,' Angus Mudie explained, passing the box to his wife who told the rest of the story.

'Fiona was distraught when she found out that the wolf was dead,' Mrs Mudie concluded a few moments later. 'She was given this sketchbook and drew all of these beautiful pictures.' She turned the delicate pages carefully.

'They're exquisite,' Emily Hope said. 'Is that Fiona?'

Mandy leaned closer as Mrs Mudie nodded, before turning the page. 'Here we are,' she said, holding it up and smiling at them. 'Here's the wolf portrait. I *knew* it couldn't be missing.'

Mandy took a breath and felt her eyes widening. Staring back at her was the old wolf.

'And these marks are where Fiona shed tears as she drew it,' Mandy heard Mrs Mudie say, but it sounded as if she were a long way away.

Somehow, Mandy thought to herself, *the old wolf knew that the young wolves were in danger. He didn't want them to be shot, as he had been, and he knew they'd need our help.* She dragged her gaze away and looked at James and Cameron. They both looked stunned too.

'Mandy, look at his eyes,' Mrs Hope called. 'She's drawn them beautifully. What a strange expression . . .'

Mandy stared at the portrait. It was all in black and white but she knew that the old wolf's eyes were a glowing yellow. His eyes had been so sad when she had first seen him at the window. But now they were very different.

'I know exactly what his expression is,' Mandy said positively. 'He looks proud!' She grinned at them all. 'The old grey wolf looks proud.'

HOUND ON THE HEATH
Animal Ark Hauntings

Lucy Daniels

Mandy and James will do anything to help an animal in distress. And sometimes even ghostly animals appear to need their help . . .

Out camping on the local heath, Mandy and James hear strange howling noises. When they investigate, they find a lonely greyhound whimpering near some old ruins. But, despite their coaxing, the dog won't come with them. The next day they hear about a mystery dog, parted from its owner and destined to howl every night until they are reunited. Can Mandy and James help the dog find peace?

COLT IN THE CAVE
Animal Ark Hauntings

Lucy Daniels

Mandy and James will do anything to help an animal in distress. And sometimes even ghostly animals appear to need their help . . .

Mandy and James are excited about their school trip to an old mine, especially as it means a trip down to the coal face! The mine itself is dark and gloomy – Mandy can't bear to think of the pit ponies who lived their whole lives underground. Suddenly she spots eyes gleaming at her out of the darkness. But when James investigates, he can't see anything. The very next night, Mandy dreams about a troubled pony. What does it mean?